TRADITIONAL TALES FROM
LONG, LONG AGO

Traditional Tales from Long, Long Ago

Illustrated by

Sue Clarke, Anna Cynthia Leplar, Jacqueline Mair,
Sheila Moxley, and Jane Tattersfield

This is a Parragon Publishing Book
This edition published in 2000

Parragon Publishing
Queen Street House
4 Queen Street
Bath BA1 1HE, UK
Copyright © Parragon 1999

Created by
The Albion Press Ltd
Spring Hill, Idbury, Oxfordshire OX7 6RU

Illustrations copyright © Sue Clarke, Anna Cynthia Leplar, Jacqueline Mair,
Sheila Moxley, Jane Tattersfield 1999

ISBN 0-75253-756-3

A copy of the British Library Cataloguing in Publication Data
is available from the British Library.

Typeset by York House Typographic, London
Printed and bound in Indonesia by APP Printing

Contents

The Leprechaun's Gold

It was Lady Day and everyone who had worked on the harvest had a holiday. The sun shone brightly, and there was a pleasant breeze, so Tom Fitzpatrick decided to go for a walk across the fields. He had been strolling for a while, when he heard a high-pitched noise, "Clickety-click, clickety-click," like the sound of a small bird chirruping.

Tom wondered what creature could be making this noise, so he crept quietly toward the sound. As he peered through some bushes, the noise stopped suddenly, and what did Tom see but a tiny old man, with a leather apron, sitting on a little wooden stool. Next to the old man was a large brown jar. The little man seemed to be repairing a miniature shoe, just large enough for his own feet. Tom could not believe what he saw.

All the stories Tom had heard about the fantastic riches of the little people came back into his mind. "If I'm careful," he said to himself, "I've got it made." And Tom remembered that you should never take your eyes away from one of the little people, otherwise they disappear.

"Good day to you," said Tom. "Would you mind telling me what's in your jar?"

"Beer, some of the best there is," said the little man.

"And where did you get it from?"

"I made it myself. You'll never guess what I made it from."

"I suppose you made it from malt," said Tom.

"Wrong!" said the leprechaun. "I made it from heather!"

"You never did! You can't make beer from heather!"

"Don't you know about the Vikings? When they were here in Ireland they told my ancestors how to make beer from heather, and the secret has been in my family ever since. But you shouldn't be wasting time asking me pointless questions. Look over there where the cows have broken into the corn field and are trampling all over the corn."

Tom started to turn round, but remembered just in time that it was a trick to make him look away from the little man. He lunged at the leprechaun, knocking over the jar of beer, and

grasped the little man in his hand. Tom was angry at being tricked, and was sad to have knocked over the beer, which he had wanted to taste. But he had the creature safe in his hand.

"That's enough of your tricks!" shouted Tom. "Show me where you keep your gold, or I'll squeeze the life out of you before you can blink!"

And Tom put on such a fearsome expression that the leprechaun began to quake with fright, and to worry that Tom might truly hurt him. So he said to Tom, "You just carry me through the next couple of fields, and I'll show you the biggest crock of gold you could imagine."

So off they went. Tom held the leprechaun tightly in his fist, so that, no matter how much he wriggled and slithered, the little man could not escape. And Tom looked straight at the tiny creature, never changing his gaze, so that the leprechaun had no chance to disappear.

They walked on and on, over fields, across ditches, and through hedges. They even had to cross a crooked patch of bog, but somehow Tom managed to get through it without once looking away from the leprechaun. Finally they arrived at a field that was full of hundreds and hundreds of turnips. The leprechaun told Tom to walk towards the middle of the field, where he pointed towards a large turnip. "You just dig under that one," said the leprechaun, "and you'll find a crock full to the brim with gold coins."

Tom had nothing to dig with. He realised that he would have to go home and get his spade. But how would he find the right turnip when he returned? Quickly, he bent down to remove one of the red ribbons holding up his gaiters, and tied the ribbon around the turnip. "Now you swear to me," he said to the little creature, "that you won't take the ribbon from that turnip before I return."

The leprechaun swore that he would not remove the ribbon,

and Tom ran home to get his spade. He ran as fast as he could, because he could not wait to unearth the leprechaun's gold.

By the time Tom ran back to the turnip field, he was quite breathless. But when he opened the gate into the field he could not believe his eyes. Across the entire field a mass of red ribbons was blowing in the breeze. The leprechaun had kept his promise. He had not taken away Tom's ribbon. Instead he had tied an identical ribbon to every single turnip in the field. Now Tom knew he would never find the leprechaun's gold. His dream of fabulous riches was over.

Tom walked sulkily back home, cursing the leprechaun as he went. And every time he passed a turnip field, he gave one of the turnips a mighty wallop with his spade.

The Horned Women

It happened five hundred or more years ago, when all well-to-do women learned how to prepare and card their wool and spin it to make yarn. One evening, a rich lady sat up late in her chamber, carding a new batch of wool. The rest of the family and all the servants had gone to bed, and the house was silent. Suddenly, the lady heard a loud knocking at the door, together with a loud, high-pitched voice shouting "Open the door! Open the door!".

The lady of the house, who did not recognise the voice, was puzzled. "Who is it?" she called.

"I am the Witch of One Horn," came the reply.

The lady, who could not hear very clearly through the thick oak door, thought that it was one of her neighbors who needed help, or one of the servants in a panic, so she rushed across the room and threw open the door. The lady was quite astonished to see a tall woman, with a single horn growing in the middle of her head. The newcomer, who was carrying a pair of carders, strode across the room, sat down, and set to work carding some of the lady's wool. She worked in silence,

but all of a sudden, she looked around the room and said,
"Where are all the others? They should be here by now."

Straightaway, there was another knock on the door.
Although she was by now rather frightened, the
lady of the house could not stop herself from crossing the
room and opening the door once more. To her surprise
another witch came into the room, this time with a pair of
horns and carrying a spinning wheel.

"Make room for me," she said. "I am the Witch of Two
Horns." And no sooner had she said this than she started to
spin, producing fine woollen yarn faster than anyone the lady
had seen before.

Again and again, there came knocks on the door, and again and again the lady felt she had to get and up and let in the newcomers. This went on until there were twelve women in the room, and each had one horn more than the previous witch. They all sat around the fire, carding and spinning and weaving, and the lady of the house did not know what to do. She wanted to get up and run away, but her legs would not let her; she wanted to scream for help, but her mouth would not open. She began to realise that she was under the spell of the horned women.

As she sat watching them, wondering what she could do, one of the witches called to her: "Don't just sit there. Get up and bake us all a cake."

Suddenly, the lady found she could stand up. She looked around for a pot to take to the well to get some water for the cake mixture, but there was nothing that she could use. One of the hags saw her looking and said to her, "Here, take this sieve and collect some water in that."

The lady knew that a sieve could not hold water, but the witches' spell made her powerless to do anything else but walk off to the well and try to fill the sieve. As the water poured through the sieve, the lady sat down and cried.

Through her sobs, the lady heard a voice. It seemed as if the spirit of the well was talking to her. "There is some clay and moss behind the well-shaft. Take them, mix them together, and make a lining for the sieve. Then it will hold water."

The lady did as she was told, and the voice spoke again. "Go back to the house, and when you come to the corner, scream three times and shout these words as loud as you can: 'The mountain of the Fenian women is all aflame.'"

Straightaway the lady's screams were echoed by the cries of the horned women. All twelve witches dashed out of the house and flew away at high speed to their mountain, Slievenamon, and the lady was released from the spell. She sighed a huge sigh of relief, but she saw quickly that the witches had made their own cake and poisoned the rest of her family. The lady turned to the well, asking the spirit "How can I help my children and servants? And what shall I do if they return here again?"

So the spirit of the well taught the lady how to protect herself if the witches should return. First she had to sprinkle on her threshold some water in which she had washed her child's feet. Next she was to take pieces of the witches' cake and place a piece in the mouth of each member of her household, to bring them back to life. Then the spirit told her to take the cloth woven by the witches, and put it into her chest. And finally she was to place a heavy oak crossbeam across the door. The lady did all these things, and waited.

Soon the twelve witches returned, screaming and howling, for they had arrived at their mountain and found no fire, and were mad for vengeance.

"Open the door! Open, foot-water!" they yelled, and their cries made people tremble in the next village.

"I cannot open," called the water, "I am all scattered on the ground."

"Open the door! Open wood and beam!" they shouted, and their noise could be heard far over the hills.

"I cannot open," said the door. "For I am fastened with a stout crossbeam."

"Open the door! Open cake that we made with our enemies'

blood!" they screamed, and their screams could be heard by the sea.

"I cannot open," said the cake. "For I am broken in pieces."

And then the witches knew that they were defeated, and flew back to their mountain, cursing the spirit of the well as they went.

The lady of the house was finally left in peace. When she went outside to see that the coast was clear, she found a cloak that one of the witches had dropped. She hung the cloak up in her room, and it was kept in her family for five hundred years, in memory of her victory over the twelve horned women.

Hudden and Dudden and Donald O'Neary

Once upon a time there were two farmers, called Hudden and Dudden. They each had a huge farm, with lush pastures by the river for their herds of cows, and hillside fields for their sheep. Their beasts always brought good prices at the market. But no matter how well they did, they always wanted more.

Between Hudden's and Dudden's land was a little field with a tiny old cottage in the middle, and in this house lived a poor man named Donald O'Neary. Donald only had one cow, called Daisy, and barely enough grass to feed her.

Although he was only poor and had but a narrow strip of farmland, Hudden and Dudden were jealous of Donald. They wanted to turf him out and divide his land between them, so that they could make their farms even bigger. And whenever the two rich farmers met up, their talk would always turn to how they could get rid of poor Donald.

One day, they were talking about this and Hudden suddenly said, "Let's kill Daisy. If he has no cow, he'll soon clear out." So, Hudden and Dudden crept quietly into Donald's cowshed, fed some poison to Daisy, and made off with all speed.

At nightfall, Donald went to the shed to check that Daisy was comfortable. The cow turned to her master, licked his hand affectionately, collapsed on to the floor, and died.

Donald was saddened at Daisy's death. But, because he was a poor fellow, he had learned long ago how to cope with hardship, and he soon began to think whether he could turn his misfortune to good use. "At least I can get some money for Daisy's hide," he thought. And then he had an idea.

The next day, Donald marched off to the fair in the nearby town, with the hide slung over his shoulder. Before he got to the fair, he stopped in a quiet spot, made some slits in the hide,

and put a penny in each of the slits. Then he chose the town's best inn, strode through the door, hung up the hide on a nail, and ordered a glass of the best whisky.

The landlord looked suspiciously at Donald's ragged clothes. "Don't worry that I can't pay you," said Donald. "I may look poor, but this hide gives me all the money I want." Donald walked over to the hide, hit it with his stick, and out fell a penny. The landlord was flabbergasted.

"What can I give you for that hide?" he asked.

"It's not for sale," replied Donald. "Me and my family have lived off that hide for years. I'm not going to sell it now." And Donald whacked the hide again, producing another penny.

Eventually, after the hide had produced several more pennies, the landlord could stand it no longer. "I'll give you a whole bag of gold for that hide!" he shouted. Donald, who could not believe his good fortune, gave in, and the deal was struck.

When Donald got home, he called on his neighbor Hudden. "Would you lend me your scales? I sold a hide at the fair today and want to work out how much I have made."

Hudden could not believe his eyes as Donald tipped the gold into his scales. "You got all that for one hide?" he asked. And as soon as Donald had gone home, he raced round to Dudden's, to tell him what had happened. Dudden could not believe that poor Donald had sold Daisy's hide for a whole bagful of gold,

so Hudden took his neighbour to Donald's hovel, so that he could see for himself. They walked straight into Donald's cottage without knocking on the door, and there was Donald sitting at the table, counting his gold.

"Good evening Hudden; good evening Dudden. You thought you were so clever, playing your tricks on me. But you did me a good turn. I took Daisy's skin to the fair, where hides are fetching their weight in gold."

The next day, Hudden and Dudden slaughtered all their cattle, every single cow and calf in their fine herds. They loaded the hides on to Hudden's cart and set off to the fair.

When they arrived, Hudden and Dudden each took one of the largest hides, and walked up and down the market square shouting "Fine hides! Fine hides! Who'll buy our fine hides?" Soon a tanner went up to Hudden and Dudden.

"How much are you charging for your hides?"

"Just their weight in gold."

"You must have been in the tavern all morning if you think I'll fall for that one," said the tanner, shaking his head.

Then a cobbler came up to them.

"How much are you charging for your hides?"

"Just their weight in gold."

"What sort of a fool do you take me for?" shouted the cobbler, and landed Hudden a punch in the belly that made him stagger backwards. People heard this commotion and

came running from all over the fair ground. One of the crowd was the innkeeper. "What's going on?" he shouted.

"A pair of villains trying to sell hides for their weight in gold," replied the cobbler.

"Grab them! They're probably friends of the con man who cheated me out of a bag of gold pieces yesterday," said the innkeeper. But Hudden and Dudden took to their heels. They got a few more punches, and some nips from the dogs of the town, and some tears in their clothes, but the innkeeper did not catch them, and eventually they ran all the way home.

Donald O'Neary saw them coming, and could not resist laughing at them. But Hudden and Dudden were not laughing. They were determined to punish Donald. Before the poor

man knew what was happening, Hudden had grabbed a sack, and Dudden had forced Donald into it and tied up the opening. "We'll carry him off to the Brown Lake and throw him in!" said Dudden.

But Hudden and Dudden were tired, with running from the town and carrying Donald, so they stopped for a drink on the way, leaving Donald, in his sack, on the inn doorstep.

Once more, Donald began to think how he could gain from his problem, and he started to scream and shout inside the sack: "I won't have her. I won't have her I tell you!" He repeated this on and on until a farmer, who had just arrived with a drove of cattle, took notice.

"What do you mean?" asked the farmer.

"The king's daughter. They are forcing me to marry the king's daughter, but I won't have her."

The farmer thought how fine it would be to marry the king's daughter, to be dressed in velvet and jewels, and never again to get up at dawn to milk the cows.

"I'll swap places with you," said the farmer. "You

can take my herd, and I will get into the sack and be taken to marry the king's daughter."

So the farmer untied the sack and let out Donald O'Neary. "Don't mind the shaking, it's just the steep palace steps. And don't worry if they curse you or call you a rogue. They are angry because I have been shouting that I don't want to marry the princess," said Donald.

Quickly, the farmer got into the sack, and Donald tied up the cord and drove away the herd of cattle. He was long gone when Hudden and Dudden came out of the inn and picked up their burden. Refreshed with their whisky, they soon arrived at the lake, threw in the sack, and returned home.

Hudden and Dudden could not believe their eyes when they arrived. There was Donald O'Neary, as large as life, with a large new herd of fine fat cattle.

Donald said, "There's lots of fine cattle down at the bottom of the lake. Why shouldn't I take some for myself? Come along with me and I will show you." When they got to the lake, Donald pointed to the reflections of the clouds in the water. "Don't you see the cattle?" he said. Greedy to own a rich herd like their neighbor, the two farmers dived headfirst into the waters of the lake. And they have never been seen since.

Munachar and Manachar

There were once two little fellows called Munachar and
Manachar. They liked to pick raspberries, but Manachar always
ate them all. Munachar got so fed up with this that he said he
would look for a rod to make a gibbet to hang Manachar.

Soon, Munachar came to a rod. "What do you want?" said
the rod. "A rod, to make a gibbet," replied Munachar.

"You won't get me," said the rod, "unless you can get an ax to
cut me." So Munachar went to find an ax. "What do you
want?" said the ax. "I am looking for an ax, to cut a rod, to
make a gibbet," replied Munachar.

"You won't get me," said the ax, "unless you can get a stone
to sharpen me." So Munachar went to find a stone. "What do
you want?" said the stone. "I am looking for a stone, to sharpen
an ax, to cut a rod, to make a gibbet," replied Munachar.

"You won't get me," said the stone, "unless you can get water to wet me." So Munachar went to find water. "What do you want?" said the water. "I am looking for water to wet a stone, to sharpen an ax, to cut a rod, to make a gibbet," replied Munachar.

"You won't get me," said the water, "unless you can get a deer who will swim me." So Munachar went to look for a deer. "What do you want?" said the deer. "I am looking for a deer, to swim some water, to wet a stone, to sharpen an ax, to cut a rod, to make a gibbet," replied Munachar.

"You won't get me," said the deer, "unless you can get a hound who will hunt me." So Munachar went to look for a hound. "What do you want?" said the hound. "I am looking for a hound, to hunt a deer, to swim some water, to wet a stone, to sharpen an ax, to cut a rod, to make a gibbet," replied Munachar.

"You won't get me," said the hound, "unless you can get some butter to put in my claw." So Munachar went to look for some butter. "What do you want?" said the butter. "I am looking for some butter to put in the claw of a hound, to hunt a deer, to swim some water, to wet a stone, to sharpen an ax, to cut a rod, to make a gibbet," replied Munachar.

"You won't get me," said the butter, "unless you can get a cat who can scrape me." So Munachar went to look for a cat.

"What do you want?" said the cat. "I am looking for a cat to scrape some butter, to put in the claw of a hound, to hunt a deer, to swim some water, to wet a stone, to sharpen an ax, to cut a rod, to make a gibbet, " replied Munachar.

"You won't get me," said the cat, "unless you can get some milk to feed me." So Munachar went to get some milk. "What do you want?" said the milk. "I am looking for some milk, to feed a cat, to scrape some butter, to put in the claw of a hound, to hunt a deer, to swim some water, to wet a stone, to sharpen an ax, to cut a rod, to make a gibbet," replied Munachar.

"You won't get me," said the milk, "unless you can bring me some straw from those threshers over there." So Munachar went to ask the threshers. "What do you want?" said the threshers. "I am looking for some straw, to give to the milk, to feed a cat, to scrape some butter, to put in the claw of a hound, to hunt a deer, to swim some water, to wet a stone, to sharpen an ax, to cut a rod, to make a gibbet," replied Munachar.

"You won't get any straw," said the threshers, "unless you

bring some flour to bake a cake from the miller next door." So Munachar went to ask the miller. "What do you want?" said the miller. "I am looking for some flour to bake a cake, to give to the threshers, to get some straw, to give to the milk, to feed a cat, to scrape some butter, to put in the claw of a hound, to hunt a deer, to swim some water, to wet a stone, to sharpen an ax, to cut a rod, to make a gibbet," replied Munachar.

"You'll get no flour ," said the miller, "unless you fill this sieve with water." Some crows flew over crying "Daub! Daub!" So Munachar daubed some clay on the sieve, so it would hold water.

And he took the water to the miller, who gave him the flour; he gave the flour to the threshers, who gave him some straw; he took the straw to the cow, who gave him some milk; he took the milk to the cat, who scraped some butter; he gave the butter to the hound, who hunted the deer; the deer swam the water; the water wet the stone; the stone sharpened the ax; the ax cut the rod; the rod made a gibbet — and when Munachar was ready to hang Manachar, he found that Manachar had BURST!

King O'Toole and his Goose

Many years ago lived a king called O'Toole. He was a great king, with a large and prosperous kingdom, and he loved to ride the length and breadth of his realm, through the woods and across the fields, hunting deer.

But as time went by the king grew old and infirm, and he could no longer ride and hunt. He became sad and bored, and did not know what to do. Then one day he saw a flock of geese flying across the sky. O'Toole admired the birds' graceful flight, and decided that he would buy his own goose, to amuse himself. The king loved to watch the goose flying around his lake, and every Friday, the bird dived into the water and caught a trout for O'Toole to eat.

The graceful flight of the goose, and the tasty fish she caught, made O'Toole happy. But one day the goose grew old like her master, and could no longer amuse the king or catch fish for him. Once more O'Toole became sad, and even thought of drowning himself in his own lake.

Then O'Toole was out walking and he saw a young man he had not met before.

"God save you, King O'Toole," said the young man.

"Good day to you," said the king. "I am King O'Toole, ruler of these parts, but how did you know my name?"

"Oh, never mind," said Saint Kavin, for it was he. "I know more than that. How is your goose today?"

"But however did you know about my goose?" said the king.

"Oh, never mind, I must have heard about it somewhere."

King O'Toole was fascinated that a total stranger should know so much about him, so he started to talk with the young man. Eventually, O'Toole asked Kavin what he did for a living.

"I make old things as good as new," said Kavin.

"So are you some sort of tinker or magician?" asked O'Toole.

"No, my trade is better than those. What would you think if I made your old goose as good as new?"

At this, the king's eyes nearly popped out of his head. He whistled loudly and the goose came waddling slowly up to her master. It seemed impossible that the young man would be able to restore the crippled creature to health.

Kavin looked at the goose. "I can help her," he said. "But I don't work for nothing. What will you give me if I can make her fly again?"

The king looked around him, thinking of the great lands and riches of his kingdom, and looked at the poor old goose. He wanted nothing more in the world than to see this creature

hale and hearty once more. Even his kingdom seemed paltry by comparison. "I will give you anything that you ask for," replied King O'Toole.

"That's the way to do business. Will you give me all the land that the goose flies over on her first flight after I make her better?"

"I will," said the king.

"Then it's a bargain," said Saint Kavin.

And with that, the saint beckoned, and the goose waddled heavily towards him, and looked up to his face, as if she was asking him what he would do next. Saint Kavin picked up the goose by her two wings, and made the sign of the cross on her back. Then he threw her into the air, saying "Whoosh!", as if he was producing a gust of wind to help her up into the sky. As soon as Kavin had thrown her up, the goose soared up into the air, beat her wings gently, and was flying, high and fast, just as she had when the king first saw her.

King O'Toole could not believe his eyes. He stared up into the sky, with his mouth open in amazement, his eyes following every beat of the goose's wings and every turn of her flight. She seemed to be flying further, and higher, and more grace- fully than ever before. Then the goose made a final turn and swooped down, to land at the king's feet, where he patted her gently on the head.

"And what do you say to me," said Saint Kavin, "for making her fly again?"

"It goes to show that nothing beats the art of man," said O'Toole.

"Anything else?" said Kavin.

"And that I am beholden to you."

"But remember your promise," went on Kavin. "Will you give me every patch of ground, every field and every forest, that she has flown over on her first flight?"

King O'Toole paused and looked at the young man. "Yes, I will," he said. "Even though she has flown over every acre of my kingdom. Even if I lose all my lands."

"That is well spoken, King O'Toole," said the young man. "For your goose would not have flown again if you had gone back on your word."

So the king showed the young man all the lands of which he was now master. He called his scribes to draw up documents to prove that the kingdom had been passed from one man to the other. And so it was that Saint Kavin made himself known at last to King O'Toole. "I am Saint Kavin in disguise. I have done all this to test you, and you have not failed the test. You have done well, King O'Toole, and I will support you and give you food, drink, and somewhere to live now that you have given up your kingdom."

"Do you mean all this time I have been talking to the greatest of the saints, while I just took you for a young lad?" said the flabbergasted O'Toole.

"You know the difference now," replied Kavin.

And Kavin was good as his word, and looked after O'Toole in his old age. But neither the king nor the goose lived long. The goose was killed by an eel when she was diving for trout, and the old king perished soon afterwards. He refused to eat his dead goose, for he said that he would not eat what Saint Kavin had touched with his holy hands.

The Story of Deirdre

Long ago in Ireland lived a man by the name of Malcolm Harper. He was a good man, with a wife, and a house, and lands of his own, but no family. One day, a soothsayer called on Malcolm, and when Malcolm found out that his visitor could see into the future, he asked if the soothsayer could foretell what the future held in store for him. The soothsayer paused, went out of the house for a few minutes to collect his thoughts and look into the future, and returned to face Malcolm.

"When I looked into the future I saw that you will have a daughter who will bring great trouble to many men in Ireland. Much blood will be spilled on her account, and three of the country's bravest heroes with lose their lives because of her."

A few years later a fine daughter was born to Malcolm's wife, and they called the girl Deirdre. Malcolm and his wife were afraid of the trouble she might bring them, so they decided to find a foster mother, who would agree to keep Deirdre away from the sight of men.

When they found a suitable foster mother, they went to a far country and raised a mound of earth, and built inside a house, which could hardly be seen from outside. And there Deirdre and her foster mother lived, unknown to the world, until the girl was sixteen years of age.

The foster mother passed on all her knowledge to Deirdre, so soon the girl could sew and spin and cook, and knew all about the plants and flowers that grew around their hidden home.

Then one foul night, when a gale was blowing and black clouds filled the sky, a hunter passed the mound where Deirdre lived. He had lost the scent of his quarry, and found himself far away from his companions. Tired and lost, he settled down by the side of the grassy hillock to rest, and soon, with his tiredness

and the oncoming dark, he fell into a deep sleep.

As he slept, the hunter dreamed that he had come upon a place where the fairies lived. It seemed that he could hear the little creatures playing their music, and he began to shout out loud, "Let me in! I am a hunter far from home, and I need warmth and shelter."

Snug inside her house, Deirdre heard the huntsman's cry. "What noise is that? It sounds as if some poor creature needs our help."

Deirdre's foster mother realised what they had heard, and tried to keep her ward away from the man outside. "Just some bird or beast looking for its mate," she replied. "Leave well alone, and it will disappear into the woods."

But Deirdre had heard the hunter asking to be let in, and, kindhearted as she was, she would not turn away a creature in peril. "Foster mother, you have taught me to be kind and considerate to others. I will let the poor creature in and give it shelter." And Deirdre unbolted the door to their house, and let the hunter come in.

When the hunter saw Deirdre, he realised that there were many men at King Connachar's court who would be overwhelmed by her beauty. He mentioned especially the great hero, Naois, son of Uisnech, who would be glad of such a wife. Although Deirdre's foster mother tried to persuade the

hunter to tell no one about the girl, he would make no such promise, and soon left, heading towards the royal palace.

As soon as he arrived at the court, he asked leave to speak to the king. "What is it you want?" asked Connachar.

"I came to tell you about the fairest woman I ever saw," replied the hunter. "Surely she must be the most beautiful in all of Ireland."

The king questioned the hunter about Deirdre, and promised him rich rewards if he would tell the king how to find her dwelling-place. Then King Connachar called for his kinsmen, and they rode off to find the place where Deirdre lived. When the king knocked at the door, the foster mother, little thinking

who it was, called out that she would only open if the king commanded her.

"This is King Connachar himself," he called, and they could do nothing but obey his command and open the door. As soon as Connachar saw Deirdre he wanted to carry her away and marry her forthwith. But Deirdre hesitated, asking the king to wait for a year and a day before their marriage. Connachar said he would wait, so long as she promised solemnly that she would marry him at the end of that time. Deirdre promised, and Connachar took her to his palace, where there were ladies-in-waiting to look after her every wish.

One day, Deirdre was out

walking with her ladies, when a group of men came past. When she saw them, Deirdre was struck with their handsome appearance, and thought that they must be Naois, son of Uisnech, and his two brothers. Deirdre could not take her eyes from Naois as he passed, and realized that she was falling in love with the young lord. Suddenly, she gathered her gown about her and began to run after the young men, leaving her ladies-in-waiting behind. "Naois, son of Uisnech," she called. "Will you leave me behind?"

When he heard Deirdre calling, Naois turned back, saw the girl, and was smitten with love himself. Swiftly, he decided to take the girl with him, and they rode away together, Naois' brothers with them, never stopping until they reached Scotland.

Naois and his brothers Allen and Arden lived in their tower, and Deirdre was happy with them, until the time came when Deirdre had promised to marry Connachar. The king began to think how he might get Deirdre back, and he decided on this plan. He would hold a great feast, inviting all the lords from his kingdom and thereabouts, including Naois and his brothers. And Connachar sent his uncle, Ferchar Mac Ro, together with Ferchar's three sons, to Scotland, to invite Naois.

Deirdre was worried when she heard Ferchar tell Naois about the king's invitation. "Do not go," she begged. "It is a

trick. I had a dream, in which I saw three hawks coming to Scotland and hovering above your tower. Their beaks were stained with red blood. They were coming for you."

But Naois insisted. "It will be bad luck for us if we do not accept the king's invitation," he said. And Ferchar Mac Ro agreed, saying, "If the king is kind to you, be kind to him in return. But if he is violent towards you, treat him in the same way. I and my three strong sons will stand by you." So Ferchar and his sons returned with Naois and his brothers. And although she was unwilling, and wept and trembled with fear, Deirdre went with them.

Once they had arrived at the palace of Connachar, Ferchar sent a message that he was back, and that Naois, Allen, Arden, and Deirdre were with him. Connachar was surprised, since he had thought that Naois would not have dared return. Because he was not yet ready to receive his guests, Connachar asked his servants to show them to a small house he kept for visitors, some way from the palace.

Connachar grew impatient and anxious about Deirdre, so he sent his kinsman Gelban Grednach down to the house to see how they fared. "Tell me whether Deirdre looks well, and whether she is still as beautiful as she was," he ordered. Gelban crept down to the house and looked in at the spy hole in the door. There was Deirdre, together with Naois

and his brothers, who were playing dice. Deirdre blushed, as she always did when someone looked at her, and Naois noticed her reddening face at once. Naois, maddened that someone should be spying on Deirdre, grabbed one of the dice and hurled it straight at the spy hole. Gelban reeled back in pain. The dice had taken out his eye. He scrambled back to the king, his hand clasped to his bleeding face.

Gelban told the king what had happened, adding that Deirdre was so beautiful he almost risked losing the sight in his other eye.

Connachar realised that he should lose no time, if Naois would ruin the sight of any man who even looked at Deirdre.

So straightaway he gathered together his three hundred bravest men, and they vowed to take Deirdre and kill her captors.

When Connachar and his men arrived, Ferchar's sons came to the aid of Naois, as they had promised. Never before was there such a fearsome sight, as the sons of Ferchar fought all comers, slashing left and right with their swords, and killing every one of Connachar's men. The king could hardly control his wrath as Naois, his brothers, and Deirdre made their escape, and the sons of Ferchar left to tell their father all about their great deeds of heroism.

Connachar had almost given up hope when he remembered his best magician, Duanan Gacha Druid. "You are supposed to be the most powerful magician in Ireland," the king said. "I have spent sacks of gold on books of spells for you and on ingredients for your magic potions, yet still my enemies escape from me. What can you do?"

"I will find a way to stop them," replied the wizard, lifting up his arms and pointing towards the middle distance. Suddenly a vast, dense forest appeared, with trees, briars, and underbrush

blocking the way of the sons of Uisnech. But Naois and Allen and Arden hacked their way through the middle of the trees, and Deirdre followed, holding Naois' hand.

"It's hopeless," said Connachar. "They can get through the trees with hardly a moment's hesitation. Surely we are powerless to stop them escaping."

"Then I will find another way to stop them," proclaimed the magician, lifting his arms once more. This time, instead of a grass-covered plain in front of the sons of Uisnech, there was a grey sea. But Naois and Allen and Arden took off their outer clothes and each man tied them in a bundle on his back. Naois lifted Deirdre and put her on his shoulders. Then the three men began to wade steadily through the great grey sea, walking further and further away from Connachar.

"They are still getting away," moaned the king. "Have you no other powers to stop them in their tracks?"

"I have yet one more way to stop them," cried the druid, gesturing with his arms yet again. And no sooner had the druid raised his arms than the sea began to freeze. Each wave was as sharp as a sword on one side, and the other side was coated with deadly poison. It seemed that no living thing would be able to pass through.

Arden was the first to be overcome. Naois lifted him above the frozen waves, but Arden was already dying. Soon Allen too was feeling faint, and perished before Naois could do anything to help him. When he saw his two beloved brothers dead beside him, Naois too gave up hope. With his brothers gone he little cared whether he was alive or dead, and soon he was overcome by the deadly frozen sea.

"All the sons of Uisnech are gone," said the druid. "You may take your rightful wife."

But hard as he looked, Connachar could no longer see Deirdre. "Take away the frozen waves, so that I can see if she still lives," commanded the king. The druid's magic took away the sea, and there was the green plain once more. In the centre were the three dead sons of Uisnech, and by their side was Deirdre, her head bowed in mourning for the death of Naois, the man she truly loved.

Connachar ordered graves to be dug for the three brothers, and Deirdre followed them, still sorrowing, to the burial place. When she arrived, she told the gravediggers to make the grave larger and wider, until she jumped into the grave beside the body of Naois, and died by his side.

The king told his men to take her body out of the grave and buried it well away, on the opposite shore of the loch. But as time went by, a fir tree grew above the grave of Naois, and another over Deirdre's grave. Slowly, the two trees grew together, until their branches met above the loch's waters. Connachar did not like to be reminded of the love of Naois and Deirdre, so ordered the branches to be cut. Again, the branches grew, and again they were removed. But the time came when Connachar took a new wife, and she told him to let the branches grow over the waters as they would, and to leave the dead to lie in peace.

Stuck for a Story

There was once a king of Leinster whose favourite pastime was listening to stories. Every evening, before the king went to sleep, he called his best storyteller to him, and the storyteller told him a story, a different one each night. And whatever problems or worries had troubled the king during the day, they were eased away by the skill of the storyteller, and the king always had a good night's sleep. In return, the king granted his storyteller a large estate, with a big house and acres of land, for he thought that the storyteller was one of the most important men in his entire kingdom.

Each morning, when the storyteller got up, he went for a walk around his estate before breakfast and thought up his story for the evening. But one morning, after walking around his whole estate, he found it impossible to think of a new tale. He seemed to be unable to get beyond "There was once a king of Ireland" or "In olden times there was a great king with three sons."

His wife called the storyteller in to breakfast, but he said he would not come in until he had thought of a story. Then, as she was calling him again, he saw an old, lame beggarman in the distance, and went up to talk to him.

"Good morning to you. Who might you be, and what are you doing here?" asked the storyteller.

"Never mind who I am," replied the old man. "I was resting awhile, for my leg is painful and I am tired, wondering who would play a game of dice with me."

The storyteller thought that a poor old man would have little money to gamble with. But the beggar said he had a hundred gold pieces, and the storyteller's wife said, "Why don't you play with him? A story might come to you afterward." And so the two men began to throw.

Things did not go well for the storyteller. Soon he had lost all his money, but the old man still asked him to play another game. "I have no money left," said the storyteller.

"Then play for your chariot and horses and hounds," said the old man. The storyteller was unwilling to gamble away his possessions, but his wife encouraged him to take the risk.

"Go on, play another game, you might win. And anyway I don't mind walking." So they threw the dice, and again the storyteller lost the game.

"Will you play again," said the old man.

"Don't make fun of me," said the storyteller. "I have nothing to stake."

"Then play for your wife," said the beggar. Once again, the storyteller was unwilling, and turned his back on the beggar, but again his wife encouraged him, so they played and the storyteller lost once more.

The storyteller's wife went to join the beggar.

"Have you anything else to stake?" asked the old man. When the storyteller remained silent, the old man said simply, "Stake yourself."

They rolled the dice for the final time, and yet again the story teller was the loser. "You have won me," said the storyteller. "Now what will you do with me?"

"What kind of animal would you prefer to be, a fox, a deer, or a hare?"

The storyteller thought, and decided that he would rather be a hare, for at least he would be able to run away from danger. So the old man took a wand out of his pocket and turned the storyteller into a hare. Then his wife called her hounds, and they chased the hare, round and round the field, and all along the high stone wall that ran around it. And all the while the beggar and the storyteller's wife laughed and laughed to see the hare twist, turn, and double back on his path to try to avoid the hounds. The hare tried to hide behind the wife, but

she just kicked him back into the field. The hounds were about to catch him when the beggar waved his wand, the hounds fell back, and the storyteller reappeared in the hare's place.

When the beggar asked the storyteller how he liked the hunt, the storyteller said he wished he was a hundred miles away. Suddenly, the beggar waved his wand, and the storyteller found himself in a different part of the country, at the castle of the lord Hugh O'Donnell. What was more, the storyteller realised quickly that he was invisible—he could see all about him, but no one could see him.

Soon the beggar arrived at O'Donnell's castle.

"Where have you come from and what do you do?" asked the lord.

"I am a great traveler and magician," said the beggar.

Soon, the beggar was playing tricks on O'Donnell's men. "Give me six pieces of silver and I will show you that I can move one of my ears without moving the other."

"Done," said one of O'Donnell's men. "You'll never move one ear without moving the other, even great ears like yours!"

The beggarman then put one hand to one of his ears, and gave it a sharp pull.

O'Donnell roared with laughter, and paid the beggar six pieces of silver for the joke. But his man was less pleased.

"What sort of trick do you call that?" he said. "Any fool could move his ear that way." And the man gave his own ear a mighty pull—and off came ear and head together.

Everyone in the castle was dumbstruck, except for the beggar, who said, "Now I'll show you an even better trick." He took out of his bag a ball of silk, unrolled it, and threw it up into the air, where it turned into a thick rope. Then he sent a hare racing up the rope, followed by a hound to chase it.

"Who will catch the hound and stop it eating my hare?" challenged the beggar. Sure enough, one of O'Donnell's men ran up the rope, and everyone below waited. When nothing had happened for a while, the beggar said, "It looks as if he has fallen asleep and let the dog eat the hare."

The beggar began to wind up the rope, and sure enough,

there was the man fast asleep and the hound polishing off the hare. The old beggar looked angry that the man had failed in his task, drew his sword, and beheaded both man and hound.

O'Donnell was enraged that two of his men, and one of his best hounds, had been beheaded in his own castle. He went to seize the beggar, but the old man put up his hand. "Give me ten pieces of silver for each of them, and they shall be cured."

No sooner had O'Donnell paid over the silver, than men and hound were restored to their former health. As for the beggar, he had vanished, taking the invisible story teller with him.

To the story teller's relief he

found himself back at the court of the King of Leinster, with the beggar beside him. But his relief did not last long. The king was looking for his storyteller, and instead here was the old beggar, who started to insult the royal harpers. "Their noise is worse than a cat purring over its food, or buzzing honey-bees," said the beggar.

"Hang the man who insults my harpers," shouted the king.

But when the king's guards took him off to be hanged, the beggar escaped, and they found that the king's favorite brother was mysteriously hanged in his place.

"Hang the right man this time!" bawled the king.

But this time the king's best harper was found on the gibbet.

"Do you want to try hanging me again?" grinned the beggar.

"Get out!" roared the king.

But before he went, the beggar made the storyteller visible again, and gave him back his chariot, his horses, his hounds— and his wife. "I had heard you were in difficulties," he said to the storyteller. "Now you have the story of your adventures to tell the king." Sure enough, the king thought the new story was the best he had ever heard. From that day on, it was the tale the king always wanted to hear, and the storyteller never had to think up a new story again.

The Legend of Knockgrafton

By the Galtee mountains long ago lived a poor basket-maker. He always wore a sprig of foxglove in his straw hat, so everyone called him Lusmore, an old Irish name for the foxglove. The most noticeable thing about Lusmore was that he had a huge hump on his back. This hump was so large that his head pressed down and his chin rested on his chest.

When they first saw Lusmore, most people were scared of him. But when they got to know him, they realised that he was one of the most charming and helpful of people. People were surprised that he was so sweet-tempered, since he had to bear such a deformity.

One day, Lusmore had been to a nearby town to sell some baskets, and he was walking back home. He could only go quite slowly, and found himself by the ancient mound at Knockgrafton as it got dark. He still had a way to travel, so decided to sit down beside the mound and rest for a while.

As soon as he sat down, Lusmore began to hear the most beautiful, unearthly music. He had never heard anything so

56

melodious before, with many voices singing different words, but blending in perfect harmony. Stranger still, the sound seemed to be coming from within the mound.

Lusmore was enchanted with the music which came from the mound, and eventually started to sing along with it, adding his own strain which blended beautifully with the music, making it sound even better than before. Suddenly, Lusmore found himself picked up at lightning speed, and before he knew what had happened, he was inside the mound. All around Lusmore danced tiny fairies, obviously delighted that he had liked their singing and added his own voice to their song.

Round and round they danced, in constant movement in time to the melodious song, and Lusmore smiled in amazement and enjoyment.

When the song was finally over, Lusmore watched the group of fairies start to talk among themselves, occasionally glancing up at him before going back to their conversation. He felt rather frightened, wondering what they would do to him now that he had seen inside their secret home. Then one fairy stepped out from the group and came towards him, chanting, "Lusmore, Lusmore, The hump that you bore, You shall have it no more, See it fall to the floor, Lusmore, Lusmore!".

Lusmore felt lighter, and he seemed to be able to move more easily. In fact, he felt as if he could jump to the Moon and back. Slowly, he started to lift his head, and, yes, he could stand up straight, straighter than he had ever stood before. It was true! The hump was gone!

As he looked around him, noticing again the strange beauty of the fairies who had been so kind to him, Lusmore began to feel dizzy. Then a tiredness came upon him and he fell asleep amongst the fairies.

When Lusmore awoke, he found himself outside the mound at Knockgrafton, and the morning sun was shining brightly. He said his prayers, then moved his hand gingerly towards his back. There was still no hump, and Lusmore stood proudly up,

standing his full height for the first time. To his delight he also noticed that the fairies had left him dressed in a smart new suit of clothes. So off he went home, with a spring in his step that he had never had before.

To begin with, none of his neighbors recognized Lusmore. But when they realised that he had lost his hump, word spread quickly, and soon everyone was talking about Lusmore's amazing good fortune.

One day, Lusmore was sitting by his door working away at a new basket, when an old woman appeared.

"Good day," she said. "I am looking for a man called

Lusmore, who had his hump removed by the fairies. For my best friend's son has such a hump, and if he could visit the fairies just as Lusmore did, perhaps he too could be cured."

The basket-maker told the old woman that she had found Lusmore, and explained the story of how he had heard the fairies singing, how he had joined in their song, how his hump had been taken away, and how he had been given a new suit of clothes. And the old woman thanked Lusmore, and went back to tell her friend what her son, Jack Madden, should do to rid himself of his hump.

Straight away Jack Madden set off for the old mound at Knockgrafton, and sat down beside it. Soon he began to hear the bewitching sound of the fairies singing. In fact, the music was even sweeter than before, because the fairies had added Lusmore's part to their song. Jack Madden was in a hurry to be rid of his hump, and started joining in straightaway. Unlike Lusmore, he was a greedy fellow, who thought that if he sung louder, he might get two new suits of clothes instead of Lusmore's one. And unlike Lusmore, Jack did not listen carefully to the song, and make his own voice blend with the fairies. He bawled away as loudly as he could, almost shouting out the fairies in his eagerness to be heard.

Just as he expected, Jack Madden was taken inside the mound and surrounded by fairies. But the fairies were angry with Jack

Madden. "Who was spoiling our song?" they cried. And one of the fairies started to chant at Jack Madden:

"Jack Madden, Jack Madden, You are such a bad'un, Your life we will sadden, Two humps for Jack Madden!"

And a group of fairies took Lusmore's old hump and stuck it on Jack's back.

When Jack Madden's mother and her friend came to the mound to look for Jack, they found him with his two humps. Although they pulled and pulled at the new hump, they could not remove it. They went home cursing the fairies and anyone who dared to go and listen to fairy music. And poor Jack Madden had two humps for the rest of his life.

A Donegal Fairy

There was once an old woman who lived in Donegal, and she was boiling a large pot of water over the fire. The water was just starting to boil when suddenly, one of the little people slid down the chimney and fell with one leg in the hot water.

He screamed a piercing scream, and the old lady looked on in wonder as dozens of tiny fairies quickly appeared around the fireplace and pulled him out of the water.

One of the rescuers pointed suspiciously towards the old woman. "Did the old wife scald you?" said the tiny figure, with a menacing tone in his voice.

"No, no, it was my own fault. I scalded myself," replied the first fairy.

"Ah, just as well for her," said the rescuer. "If she had scalded you, we would have made her squeal."

The Giant's Causeway

In ancient times, when giants lived in Ireland, there were two who were the strongest and most famous giants of them all, Fin M'Coul and Cucullin. Cucullin rampaged all over Ireland, fighting with every giant he met, and always coming out the winner. People said that Cucullin could make an earthquake by stamping on the ground, and that he once flattened a thunderbolt into a pancake, and carried it around in his pocket. They said that his strength lay in the middle finger of his right hand. Fin was strong too, but he was secretly afraid of Cucullin, and whenever he heard that the other giant was coming near, Fin found some excuse to move on.

It happened at one time that Fin and his relatives were away working on the Giant's Causeway, a great road that they were building over the sea to link Ireland and Scotland. As they worked, word reached Fin that Cucullin was on his way. "I think I'll be off home for a while to see my wife Oonagh," said Fin. "She misses me when I go away to work."

So Fin set off to his home on top of the hill at Knockmany. Many people wondered why Fin and Oonagh lived there. It

was a long climb up and they had to carry their water to the top. Fin said he chose the place because he liked the view. In truth, he lived there so that he could see whether Cucullin was coming. And Knockmany was the best lookout for miles around, higher than any hill in the region except for the nearby hill of Cullamore, where Oonagh's sister Granua lived.

As Fin embraced Oonagh, she asked him, "What brought you home so early, Fin?"

"I came home to see you, my love," said Fin, and the couple went in happily to eat.

Oonagh had not been long with her husband when she realised that he was worried, and she guessed that there was some other reason for his return.

"It's this Cucullin that's troubling me," admitted Fin. "He can make the earth shake by stamping his foot, and he can squash thunderbolts into pancakes. The beast is coming to get me. If I run away, I will be disgraced; if I stay, he'll squash me like a pancake. I don't know what I'm going to do."

"Well, don't despair," said his wife. "Maybe I can get you out of this scrape." And Fin wondered what she was going to do.

First of all, Oonagh called across to her sister Granua, on the neighboring hill of Cullamore. "Sister, what can you see?" she shouted.

"I can see the greatest giant I ever saw. He is coming this way and has just walked through Dungannon. I will call him up my hill and offer him refreshment. That may give you and Fin some more time to prepare for him."

Meanwhile, Fin was getting more and more nervous. All he could think of was the thunderbolt, flattened like a pancake in Cucullin's pocket, and he trembled with fear at what might become of them.

"Be easy, Fin," said Oonagh. "Your talk of pancakes has given me an idea. I am going to bake some bread."

"What's the point of baking bread at a time like this?" wailed Fin.

But Oonagh ignored him, and started mixing the dough, singing quietly to herself, as if she had not a care in the world. She then went out to visit her neighbors, something that made Fin even more anxious. She did not seem to be giving a thought to the giant Cucullin.

When Oonagh returned, she was carrying twenty-one iron griddles, which she had borrowed from her neighbours. She went back to her work and kneaded each iron griddle into a portion of the dough, to make twenty-one bread cakes, each with a hard iron griddle in the centre. Oonagh baked the bread cakes in the fire, and put them away in her cupboard when they were done. Then she sat down to rest, and smiled contentedly.

On the following day, they finally spied Cucullin coming up the hill towards their house. "Jump into bed," said Oonagh to Fin. "You must pretend to be your own child. Don't say any-thing, but listen to what I say, and be guided by me."

At two o'clock, as they expected, Cucullin arrived. "Is this the house of Fin M'Coul?" he asked. "I have heard talk that he says he is the strongest giant in all Ireland, but I want to put him to the test."

"Yes, this is his house, but he is not here. He left suddenly in great anger because someone told him that a great beast of a giant called Cucullin was in the neighborhood, and he set out

at once to catch him. I hope he doesn't catch the poor wretch, for if he does, Fin will surely knock the stuffing out of him."

"Well I am that Cucullin," replied the giant. "And I have been searching for him. He will be sorry when I find him, for I shall squash him like a pancake."

Fin began to tremble when he heard the dreaded word "pancake", but Oonagh simply laughed.

"You can't have seen Fin," she said. "For if you had, you would think differently. But since you are here, perhaps you could help me. You'll notice that the wind is blowing at the door and making a terrible draft. Turn the house round for me, as Fin would have done if he were here."

Cucullin could hardly believe that Fin had the strength to turn the whole house around. But he went outside, grasped the building in his hand, pulled hard, and moved it around, so that the wind no longer blew at the door.

"Now, Fin was telling me that he was going to crack those cliffs on the hill down below, to make a spring come up and bring us water. Will you do that for me, since Fin is not here to do it himself?" Again, Cucullin was astonished at Fin's strength, and went outside to make a crack in the rocks for the water to come through.

Oonagh thanked him for the trouble he had taken, and offered him some food for his pains. And out with the meat and cabbage, she brought one of the bread cakes she had baked. When Cucullin bit on the bread, he cried out in pain, "Aagh! That's two of my best teeth broken!" he wailed.

"But that's the only bread that my husband will eat," said Oonagh. "Try another cake. It may not be so hard."

The hungry giant grabbed another, but his hand flew to his mouth in horror: "The Devil take your bread, or I'll have no teeth left!" he roared.

Oonagh pretended to be surprised. "Even our son eats this bread," she said, passing Fin a bread cake with no iron inside.

By now Cucullin was shaking in terror. If the young lad was so strong he could eat bread like this, what would his father be like? Cucullin decided he would be off before Fin came home. But he could not resist asking to look at the teeth of the child that could eat bread with iron inside.

"It's the back teeth that are the strongest," said Oonagh. "Put your finger into the child's mouth, and feel for yourself."

Cucullin slipped his middle finger into Fin's mouth, and Fin knew his chance had come. Fin bit hard on the giant's finger, and when Cucullin pulled his hand away in surprise, the middle finger was gone. Cucullin was crushed. He knew his strength was gone with his finger, and he ran from the house, screaming and roaring, and they never saw him again.

Fair, Brown, and Trembling

Once upon a time long ago lived King Hugh Curucha, and he had three daughters called Fair, Brown, and Trembling. Fair and Brown were his favourite daughters. They were always given new dresses and were allowed to go to church every Sunday. But Trembling, who was the most beautiful of the three, had to stay at home, where she did the cooking and housework. The other two forced Trembling to stay at home like this because they were jealous of her beauty, and feared that she might attract a husband before them.

After Trembling had been kept at home like this for seven years, the Prince of Emania met Fair, the eldest of the sisters, and fell in love with her. Just after this had happened, Fair and Brown went off to church as usual and Trembling stayed at home to cook dinner. As she worked, she talked to the old Henwife, the woman who kept the chickens on the royal farm, who had called at the kitchen. "Why haven't you gone to church too?" asked the Henwife.

"I cannot go to church," replied Trembling. "All my clothes are in tatters. Besides, if I dared to go to church, my sisters would beat me for leaving the house."

"If you could have a new dress," said the Henwife, "what sort of dress would you choose?"

"I would like a dress as white as the snow, with a pair of bright green shoes to go with it," replied Trembling.

Then the Henwife put on her cloak, snipped a tiny piece of cloth from the dress Trembling was wearing, and asked for the most beautiful white dress, and a brand new pair of green shoes. Straight away, a long white dress appeared in the old woman's hands, and a pair of green shoes, and she gave them to Trembling, who put them on. Then the Henwife gave the girl a honey-bird to put on her shoulder, and led her to the door. There stood a fine white horse, with a saddle and bridle

richly decorated with gold.

"Off you go to church," said the Henwife. "But when you get there, do not go inside, be sure to stand just outside the church door. As soon as the people start to leave at the end of Mass, be ready to ride off as quickly as you can."

So Trembling rode to church, and stayed by the door as the old woman had told her. Even though she remained outside, many people within caught a glimpse of her, and began to wonder who she was. At the end of Mass, several people ran out to get a better look at her, but she turned her horse and galloped away at great speed, so no one could catch her.

As she entered the kitchen, Trembling began to worry that no one had finished cooking dinner for her sisters. But she saw straight away that the Henwife had cooked the meal, and Trembling put on her old dress as quickly as she could.

When Fair and Brown returned, they were full of talk about the mysterious lady in white whom they had seen outside the church door. They demanded that their father buy them fine white dresses like the lady's, and next Sunday, they wore their new dresses to church.

Again, the Henwife appeared in the kitchen, and asked Trembling if she wanted to go to church. This time the old woman produced a black satin dress, with red shoes for Trembling's feet. With the honey-bird on her shoulder, she rode on a black mare

with a silver saddle, and stayed quietly by the door of the church.

The people in the church were even more amazed when they saw the strange lady by the door. Everyone wondered who she could be, but Trembling gave them no chance to find out, and rode away as soon as Mass was over.

Back home, Trembling removed her fine robe as she had before, and put the finishing touches to the meal prepared by the Henwife. When Fair and Brown arrived home from church, they were full of talk about the fine lady and her black satin dress. "No one even noticed our fine dresses," complained Fair. "They were too busy admiring the lady by the church

door and wondering who she might be. Everyone was staring at her with their mouths open, and none of the men even glanced at us!"

Fair and Brown would give their father no peace until he bought them fine black satin dresses, just like the one they had seen their sister wearing, and red shoes to go with them. Of course, Fair and Brown's dresses were not as elegant nor as finely made as Trembling's gown. They could not find one to match it anywhere in Ireland.

Off went Fair and Brown next Sunday in their new black dresses, and yet again the Henwife turned to Trembling and asked her what she wanted to wear to church. "I would dearly like a rose-red dress, a green cape, a hat with feathers of red, white and green, and shoes of the same colors."

The Henwife smiled to think of the fantastic mixture of colors that Trembling had chosen, but once more did her magic, and quickly Trembling was dressed in the garments of her choice, and mounted on a mare with diamond-shaped spots of white, blue, and gold over her body. The honey-bird began to sing as Trembling rode off to church, to wait outside the door.

By this time, news had spread all over Ireland about the beautiful lady who waited outside the church every Sunday, and many lords and princes had come to see her for themselves. Amongst them was the Prince of Emania, who, once he had seen Trembling, forgot all about her elder sister, and vowed to catch the strange lady before she could ride away. At the end of Mass, the prince sprinted out of church, and ran behind Trembling's mare. He was just able to grab hold of one of her shoes, before she galloped away into the distance.

The Prince of Emania vowed that he would search the length and breadth of Ireland until he found the woman whose foot would fit the shoe in his hand. The other princes joined him, as they too were curious, and they searched in every town and village until they came to the house of Fair, Brown, and Trembling. Both Fair and Brown tried to force their feet into

the shoe, but it was too small for them. The prince asked if there was any other woman in the house. Trembling began to speak up, but Fair and Brown tried to stop her.

"Oh, she is just a serving-girl we keep to clean the house," said Fair. But the prince insisted that every woman should have the chance to try on the shoe.

When the shoe fitted exactly the prince was overjoyed. He was about to declare his love, when Trembling begged him to wait. She ran very quickly to the house of the Henwife, who helped Trembling on with her white dress; then she returned home to show everyone that she was truly the mysterious lady. She then did the same thing with the other dresses, amazing her sisters more and more each time. The princes were just as surprised, and before she had put on the third dress, they were all challenging the Prince of Emania to fight for her hand.

The Prince of Emania fought bravely, defeating the Prince of Lochlin, who fought him for nine hours, the Prince of Spain, who fought for eight hours, and the Prince of Greece, who fought for seven hours. And at the end no one would fight the Prince of Emania, for they knew he would be the winner. So the Prince of Emania married Trembling, and the celebrations lasted for a year and a day.

All seemed to be going happily, but Fair was still very jealous of her sister. So one day, she called on her sister, and the two walked by the coast. When they came to the sea, Fair waited until there was no one to see her, then pushed Trembling into the water. Just as it seemed Trembling would drown, a great whale came and swallowed her up. When Fair returned to the prince she put on her sister's clothes and pretended to be Trembling. But even though the two were as alike as could be, the Prince was not fooled by her trick.

Now Fair thought that no one had seen her push her sister into the sea, but a young cow-boy had watched the two sisters from a nearby field. Next day he was again in the field when he saw the whale swim by and throw Trembling out upon the sand.

Then Trembling spoke to the cow-boy, saying "Run home and tell the prince my husband what has happened. If he does not come and shoot the whale, it will carry on swallowing me, and casting me out, while keeping me under a spell. I will never be able to leave the beach and come home."

The cow-boy ran to tell the Prince what had happened, but the elder sister stopped him in his tracks, and gave him a potion to drink. The drink made him forgetful, and he said nothing about what he had seen. The next day the cow-boy returned to the sea, and once more saw the whale cast out Trembling on the shore. Trembling asked the boy if he had taken her message to the Prince and the boy admitted that he had forgotten. Shamefully, he ran to tell the prince, and again Fair gave him the potion. On the third day, when the cow-boy was by the sea and saw Trembling cast out yet again, the girl guessed what had happened and spoke to him, saying "Do not let her give you any drink when you go home. She is using a potion to make you forget what has happened."

And so it was that the prince was finally brought news of his wife. He ran to the shore, loaded his gun, and shot the whale, releasing Trembling from the creature's spell. From then on the cow-boy lived in the Prince's household, and when he came of age, he married Trembling's daughter. They all lived happily, for many years, until the Prince and Trembling died, contented, of old age.

The Haughty Princess

There was once a king who had a daughter. She was very beautiful and many dukes, earls, princes, and even kings came from all around to ask for her hand in marriage. But the princess was a proud, haughty creature who would have none of them. As each suitor approached her, she would find fault with him, and send him packing, usually with a rude remark which meant that the suitor was sure to have nothing more to do with her.

One of her suitors was plump, and to him she said, "I shall not marry you, Beer Belly." Another had a pale face, and to him she said, "I shall not marry you, Death-Mask." A third suitor was tall and thin, and to him she said, "I shall not marry you, Ramrod." Yet another prince had a red complexion, and to him she said, "I shall not marry you, Beetroot." And so it went on, until every unmarried duke and earl and prince, and even king, for miles around had been rejected, and her father thought she would never find a man she liked.

Then one day a prince arrived who was so handsome, and so polite, that she found it hard to find any fault with him at all.

But still the princess's pride got the better of her, and in the end, she looked at the brown curling hairs under his chin and said, somewhat reluctantly, "I shall not marry you, Whiskers".

The poor king was at his wit's end with his daughter, and finally lost his temper with her. "I'm sick of your rudeness. Soon no one will come to visit me for fear of what you will say to them. I shall give you to the first beggar who calls at our door for alms, and good riddance to you!"

Soon a poor beggar knocked at the door. His clothes were tattered and torn, his hair dirty and matted, and his beard long and straggling. Sure enough, the king called for the priest, and married his daughter to the bearded beggar. She cried and

screamed and tried to run away, but there was nothing for it.

After the ceremony, the beggar led his bride off into a wood. When she asked where they were going, he told her that the wood and all the land around belonged to the king she had called Whiskers. The princess was even sadder that she had rejected the handsome king, and hung her head in shame when she saw the poor, tumbleddown shack where the beggar lived. The place was dirty and untidy, and there was no fire burning in the grate. So the princess had to put on a plain cotton dress, help her husband make the fire, clean the place, and prepare them a meal.

Meanwhile, the beggar gathered some twigs of willow, and after they had eaten, the two sat together making baskets. But the twigs bruised the princess's fingers, and she cried out with the pain. The beggar was not a cruel man, and saw that he must find some other work for her to do, so he gave her some cloth and thread, and set her to sewing. But although the princess tried hard, the needle made her fingers bleed, and

again tears came to her eyes. So
the beggar bought a basket full
of cheap earthenware pots and
sent her to market to sell them.

The princess did well at market on the first day, and
returned with a profit. But the
next morning, just after she had
set out her wares, a drunken
huntsman came riding through
the market place, and his
mount kicked its way through
all the princess's pots. She returned to her husband in tears.

In the end, the beggar spoke to the cook at the palace of
King Whiskers, and persuaded her to give his wife a job as a
kitchen maid. The princess worked hard, and every day the
cook gave her leftovers from the table to take home for her
husband. The princess liked the cook, and got on quite well in
the kitchen, but she was still sorry she had rejected King
Whiskers.

A while later, the palace suddenly got busier. It turned out
that King Whiskers was getting married. "Who is going to
marry the king?" asked the princess. But no one knew who
the bride was going to be.

Because they were curious, the princess and the cook decided to go and see what was going on in the great hall of the palace. Perhaps they would catch a glimpse of the mysterious bride. The princess opened the door quietly and the two of them peeped in.

King Whiskers himself was in the room, and strode over when he saw the door begin to open. "Spying on the king?" he said, looking hard at the princess. "You must pay for your nosiness by dancing a jig with me." The king took her hand, led her into the room, and all the musicians began to play. But as they whirled around, puddings and portions of meat began to fly out of her pockets, and everyone in the room roared with laughter. The princess began to run to the door, but the king caught her by the hand and took her to one side.

"Do you not realise who I am?" he asked her, smiling kindly. "I am King Whiskers, and your husband the beggar, *and* the drunken huntsman who broke your pots in the market place. Your father knew who I was when he let me marry you, and we arranged all this to rid you of your pride."

The princess was so confused she did not know what to say or do. All sorts of emotions, from joy to embarrassment, welled up inside her, but the strongest of all these feelings was love for her husband, King Whiskers. She laid her head on his shoulder, and began to cry.

When she had recovered, some of the palace maids led her away and helped her put on a fine dress fit for a queen. She went back to join her husband, and none of the guests realized that the new queen was the poor kitchen maid who had danced a jig with the king.

The Man Who Never Knew Fear

There were once two brothers, called Lawrence and Carrol. Lawrence was known as the bravest boy in the village and nothing made him afraid. Carrol, on the other hand, was fearful of the least thing, and would not even go out at night.

When their mother died, they had to decide who would watch her grave. In those days it was the tradition that when a person had died, their relatives would take it in turns to stand guard over the grave, to protect it from robbers.

Carrol, who did not want to watch his mother's grave at night, made a bet with his brother. "You say that nothing makes you afraid, but I bet you will not watch our mother's tomb tonight."

Lawrence replied, "I have the courage to stay there all night." He put on his sword and marched boldly to the graveyard, where he sat down on a gravestone next to his mother's tomb.

At first, all went well, but as the night went on, the young man became drowsy. He was almost dropping off to sleep, when he saw the most awesome sight. A huge black head was coming towards him. It seemed to float through the air, and Lawrence realised that there was no body attached to it. Without taking his eye from the head, Lawrence quickly drew his sword and held it out in front of him, ready to strike if the thing came any closer. But it did not, and Lawrence stayed, looking straight at the head, until dawn.

When he got home, Lawrence told Carrol what he had seen. "Were you afraid?" asked Carrol.

"Of course I wasn't," replied Lawrence. "You know very well that nothing in the world will frighten me."

"I bet you will not watch another night," taunted Carrol.

"I would, but I have missed a whole night's sleep. You go tonight, and I will watch the third night."

But Carrol would not go, so Lawrence slept in the afternoon, and went off to the graveyard at dusk. Around midnight, a huge black monster appeared and started to scratch about near his mother's grave. Lawrence drew his sword and chopped the monster up. The graveyard was peaceful until daybreak.

Carrol was waiting for his brother to come home. "Did the great head come again?" he asked.

"No, but a monster came and tried to dig up mother's body," said Lawrence.

When the third and final night of watching came, a strange white creature appeared, with a man's head and long fangs. Again, Lawrence reached for his sword, but the ghost began to speak: "Do not strike. You have protected your mother's grave and shown yourself the bravest man in Ireland. Great wealth awaits one as brave as you. Go and seek it."

The next day Lawrence took the fifty pounds he had won from his brother in the bet, and set out to seek his riches. On his way he met a baker, and told him the story of his adventures in the graveyard. "I'll bet you another fifty pounds you'll be scared by the graveyard near here," said the baker. "Go there tonight, and bring me the goblet on the altar of the old

church." The baker had heard that the church was haunted, and that no one ever came out of the building alive.

In the dead of night, Lawrence strode up to the door of the church and hit it firmly with his sword. Straight out of the door charged an enormous black ram, with horns as long and sharp as scythes. In a flash, Lawrence struck out at the creature, and it fled, scattering its blood all around the church doorway. Then Lawrence took the goblet, and went to the baker.

The baker was astounded that Lawrence had returned in one piece, and they went to see the priest to tell him the news. The priest was overcome with joy. He paid the young man still more money, and straightaway prepared to say Mass in the church. And Lawrence continued his journey, searching for something that would make him afraid.

Lawrence traveled a long way through lonely countryside, and hardly saw a house all day, when he came to valley where a crowd of people were gathered. They were watching two men playing a ball game, but they seemed to be frightened. Suddenly, one of the players hurled the ball towards Lawrence, and it hit him straight in the chest. Lawrence reached to catch it, and saw that it was the head of a man. As Lawrence took hold of it, the head screeched, "Are you not afraid?"

"No I am not!" said Lawrence, and straight away the head, and the crowd of people, vanished from sight.

Lawrence carried on until he came to a town, by which time he was weary and in need of lodgings. When he explained his quest to a young man, his acquaintance pointed to a large house across the road. "If you will stay the night in there, you will find something to put fear in you. If you can stand it, I will give you fifty pounds more."

So Lawrence found himself making his lodgings inside a cold, dark cellar, waiting to see what would happen. The first night, a bull and a stallion came into the room with a fearful neighing and bellowing, and began to fight for all they were worth. The next night two great black rams fought in the room, with such screeching and howling that Lawrence thought they would wake the whole town. But still he did not feel fear.

On his third night in the old house the ghost of an old, grey

man appeared. "You are truly the bravest man in Ireland," he said. "Never, since I died twenty years ago, have I found such a hero as you. Do one thing for me, and I will lead you to your riches." The old man went on to tell Lawrence how he had once wronged an old woman called Mary Kerrigan, and how he wanted Lawrence to go to Mary and beg her forgiveness. If he did this he could buy the old house and marry the old man's daughter.

Lawrence went to Mary Kerrigan and won her forgiveness. He bought the house, and all the land around it, and married the old man's daughter. They lived happily in the house, and the ghosts never returned.

The Enchantment of Earl Gerald

Earl Gerald was one of the bravest leaders in Ireland long ago. He lived in a castle at Mullaghmast with his lady and his knights, and whenever Ireland was attacked, Earl Gerald was among the first to join the fight to defend his homeland.

As well as being a great fighter, Gerald was also a magician who could change himself into any shape or form that he wanted. His wife was fascinated by this, but had never seen Gerald change his shape, although she had often asked him to show her how he could transform himself into the shape of some strange beast. Gerald always put her off with some excuse, until one day her pleading got too much for him.

"Very well," said Earl Gerald. "I will do what you ask. But you must promise not to show any fear when I change my shape. If you are frightened, I will not be able to change myself back again for hundreds of years."

She protested that the wife of such a noble warrior, who had seen him ride into battle against fearsome enemies, would not be frightened by such a small thing, so Gerald agreed to change his shape.

They were sitting quietly in the great chamber of the castle when suddenly Gerald vanished and a beautiful goldfinch was flying around the room. His wife was shocked by the sudden change, but did her best to stay calm and keep her side of the bargain. All went well, and she watched the little bird fly out into the garden, return, and perch in her lap. Gerald's wife was delighted with the bird, and smiled merrily, when suddenly and without warning, a great hawk swooped through the open windows, diving towards the finch. The lady screamed, even though the hawk missed Gerald and crashed into the table top, where its sharp beak stuck into the wood.

The damage was done. Gerald's wife had shown her fear. As she looked down to where the goldfinch had perched, she realised that the tiny bird had vanished. She never saw either the goldfinch or Earl Gerald again.

Many hundreds of years have passed by since Earl Gerald disappeared, and his poor wife is long dead. But occasionally, Gerald may be seen. Once in seven years, he mounts his steed and is seen riding around the Curragh of Kildare. Those few who have glimpsed him say that his horse has shoes made of silver, and the story goes that when these shoes are finally worn away, Gerald will return, fight a great battle, and rule as King of Ireland for forty years.

Meanwhile, in a great cavern beneath the old castle of Mullaghmast, Gerald and his knights sleep their long sleep. They are dressed in full armor and sit around a long table with the Earl at the head. Their horses, saddled and bridled, stand ready. When the right moment comes, a young lad with six fingers on each hand will blow a trumpet to awaken them.

Once, almost one hundred years ago, Earl Gerald was on one of his seven-yearly rides and an old horse dealer was passing the cavern where Gerald's knights were still sleeping. There were lights in the cavern, and the horse dealer went in to have a look. He was amazed to see the knights in their armor, all slumped on the table fast asleep, and the fine horses waiting there. He was looking at their steeds, and thinking whether he might lead one of the beasts away to market, when he dropped

the bridle he was holding. The clattering of the falling bridle echoed in the cavern and one of the knights stirred in his slumber.

"Has the time come?" groaned the knight, his voice husky with sleep. The horse dealer was struck dumb for a moment, as the knight's voice echoed in the cave. Finally he replied.

"No, the time has not come yet. But it soon will."

The knight slumped back on to the table, his helmet giving a heavy clank on the board. The horse dealer ran away home with all the speed he could manage. And Earl Gerald's knights slept on.

The Story of the Little Bird

Once long ago in a monastery in Ireland there lived a holy man. He was walking one day in the garden of his monastery, when he decided to kneel down and pray, to give thanks to God for the beauty of all the flowers and plants and herbs around him. As he did so, he heard a small bird singing, and never before had he heard any song as sweet. When his prayers, were finished, the monk stood up and listened to the bird, and

when the creature flew away from the garden, singing as it went, he followed it.

In a while they came to a small grove of trees outside the monastery grounds, and there the bird continued its song. As the bird hopped from tree to tree, still singing all the while, the monk carried on following the little creature, until they had gone a great distance. The more the bird sang, the more the monk was enchanted by the music it made.

Eventually, the two had traveled far away from the monastery, and the monk realised that it would soon be nighttime. So reluctantly, he left the bird behind and retraced his steps, arriving back home as the sun was going down in the west. As the sun set, it lit up the sky with all the colors of the rainbow, and the monk thought that the sight was almost as beautiful and heavenly as the song of the little bird he had been listening to all afternoon long.

But the glorious sunset was not the only sight that surprised the monk. As he entered the abbey gates, everything around him seemed changed from before. In the garden grew different plants, in the courtyard the brothers had different faces, and even the abbey buildings seemed to have altered. He knew he was in the right place, yet how could all these changes have taken place in a single afternoon?

The holy man walked across the courtyard and greeted the

first monk he saw. "Brother, how is it that our abbey has changed so much since this morning? There are fresh plants in the garden, new faces amongst the brothers, and even the stones of the church seem different."

The second monk looked at the holy man carefully. "Why do you ask these questions, brother? There have been no changes. Our church and gardens have not altered since morning, and we have no new brothers here—except for yourself, for though you wear the habit of our order, I have not seen you before." And the two monks looked at each other in wonder. Neither could understand what had happened.

When he saw that the

brother was puzzled, the holy man started to tell his story. He told his companion how he had gone to walk in the monastery garden, how he had heard the little bird, and how he had followed the creature far into the countryside to listen to its song.

As the holy man spoke, the expression on the second monk's face turned from puzzlement to surprise. He said, "There is a story in our order about a brother like you who went missing one day after a bird was heard singing. He never returned to the abbey, and no one knew what befell him, and all this happened two hundred years ago."

The holy man looked at his companion and replied, "That is indeed my story. The time of my death has finally arrived. Praised be the Lord for his mercies to me." And the holy man begged the second monk to take his confession and give him absolution, for the hour of his death was near. All this was done, the holy man died before midnight, and he was buried with great solemnity in the abbey church.

Ever since, the monks of the abbey have told this story. They say that the little bird was an angel of the Lord, and that this was God's way of taking the soul of a man who was known for his holiness and his love of the beauties of nature.

The Demon Cat

In Connemara there lived a woman who was very fond of fish. She married a fisherman, and on most days he brought home a good catch. They had enough fish to sell in the market and plenty for the wife to eat. But every night a large black cat would break into their house and steal the best fish.

To begin with, the cat came only at night, and the woman could never catch it. But one day, dark storm clouds came, and the beast arrived during the daytime, as the woman and her friends were spinning. The woman's daughter looked at the cat. "That great beast must be the devil," she said. Straight away the cat scratched the girl's arm, and stood by the door to stop them escaping. "I'll teach you how to behave to a gentleman," he said.

The women began to scream, and a passing man heard them, and pushed at the door. The cat held the door closed, but the passerby managed to get his stick through and gave the cat a hefty blow. The beast would have none of this, and jumped up to scratch the man's face. Blood flew everywhere, and the man ran off, scared out of his wits.

"Now I'll have my dinner," said the cat, once more taking the biggest fish. And when the women tried to hit it, it scratched and tore at them, and they ran away in terror.

When she had got her breath back, the fisherman's wife decided on a new plan. She went to the priest, asked for some holy water, and returned home. Walking on tiptoe, she entered her house, and there was the cat, helping himself to more fish. Silently she sprinkled holy water on to the beast, and thick black smoke rose up from its fur. Soon the cat began to shrivel up, and only the animal's two red eyes could be seen, staring through the blackness. Then the animal's remains disappeared, and the smoke began to clear away. The woman knew that the demon cat would trouble her no more.

The Maiden from the Lake

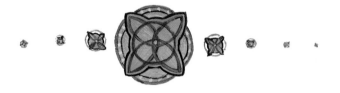

There was once a shepherd who lived in Myddvai, by the mountains of Caermarthen. A great lake was near his pastures, and one day he was watching his sheep near its shores when he saw three beautiful maidens rise from the waters. The young women came to the shore, shook the water from their hair, and walked around among the sheep.

The shepherd was overcome by the beauty of the maiden who came nearest to him, and he offered her some bread from his pack. The girl took the bread, tried a little, and said to the shepherd, "Your bread's too hard. You won't catch me." Then she ran back to the lake with the others.

The shepherd wondered whether he would see the maidens again, but just in case, on the next day, he brought some bread that was not so well baked. To his delight, the maidens appeared again, and he offered the softer bread. But this time the girl said, "Your bread's not baked. You won't catch me." Once more, she returned to the water.

On the third day, the shepherd waited for the young woman. When she came, he offered her some bread that had been

102

floating on the water. This she liked, and the couple talked for
a long while. Finally, the maiden agreed to marry the shepherd,
but gave this warning: she would be a good wife to him, as
good as any ordinary Welsh woman, unless he struck her three
times without reason. The shepherd vowed that he would
never do this, and the couple were soon married.

The shepherd and his bride were happy, and in time had
three fine sons. It happened that they were going to christen
one of the children when the wife said that it was too far to
walk to church.

"Then go and get the horses," said the shepherd, "and we will
ride all the way."

"While I get the horses, will you fetch my gloves from the
house?" asked his wife.

But when the shepherd returned with the gloves he found that she had not fetched the horses, and he tapped her gently on the shoulder to remind her.

"That's one strike," said his wife.

A little while later, the pair were at a friend's wedding. The shepherd found his wife crying and again he tapped her on the shoulder as he asked her what was wrong.

"Trouble is coming for you," she replied. "That is the second time you have struck me without reason. Take care to avoid the third time."

From then on, the shepherd was careful not so much as to tap his wife, until one day the couple were at a funeral. All of a sudden, the wife began to laugh loudly. The shepherd was amazed. He could not understand why anyone should laugh at such a sad time, so, touching her rather roughly, he said, "Wife, why are you laughing when all around you are sad?"

"I am laughing because people who die leave their troubles behind them. But your troubles have just begun. You have struck me for a third time. Now I must make an end to our marriage and bid you farewell."

The shepherd knew that the time had come for his wife to leave him, and he was sad to the bottom of his heart. But he was still more surprised when he heard his wife calling all the cattle around her, bidding them follow her to her home

beneath the waters of the lake. He saw all his cattle, even a black calf that had recently been slaughtered and a team of oxen that were ploughing a field, get up and follow her away. The oxen even took their plough with them, cutting a deep furrow all the way to the shore.

The mark left by the plough can still be seen running across the pastures by the lake. But the lady has only been seen once more. When her sons had grown up, she returned to visit them. She gave them miraculous gifts of healing. And ever since, the Doctors of Myddvai have been famous throughout the land of Wales.

The Wooing of Olwen

Long ago lived Kilhuch, son of King Kilyth. Kilhuch was brought up by his stepmother, because his own mother died when he was a baby. And his stepmother foretold that when Kilhuch was a man he would marry a young woman named Olwen, great in beauty but difficult to win.

When Kilhuch came of age, none of his family knew Olwen. His father told him to go to the court of his cousin, King Arthur, in the hope that the king would know the lady's whereabouts, and grant his consent for Kilhuch to marry.

Kilhuch looked a brave young knight as he set off on his journey, riding a fine steed with bridle and saddle of gold and cloth of richest purple. Kilhuch carried spears of silver and a gold-hilted sword, and two greyhounds, their collars studded with rubies, followed him along the road.

Arthur gave Kilhuch a royal welcome when he arrived, and straightaway offered the young man board and lodgings with his knights. But Kilhuch explained that he had come to ask a favor of the king, not to stay at court. When Arthur heard what Kilhuch wanted, he replied, "Young man, I have never heard of Olwen, and do not know her family. But I will send my messengers out to find her." So Kilhuch remained at Arthur's court while messengers went to every part of the kingdom in search of the mysterious Olwen.

The messengers returned after a year, and none had any news of Olwen. Kilhuch, full of sadness, was preparing to leave Arthur's court, when one of the knights, Kay, came up to him. "Do not go alone," he said. "I will come with you and we will search the whole of Britain until either we find Olwen, or find that she does not exist."

Arthur saw that the two men were serious in their quest and chose a number of his knights to go with them. Bedwyr,

swiftest of the knights and firm friend of Kay, Kynthelig, the
best guide of all, Gwrhyr, who knew many languages, and
Menw, gifted with powers of enchantment – all these went
with them, and they journeyed far until they found a castle on
a broad, open plain.

They asked a shepherd and his wife about Olwen, and the
woman told them that Olwen lived nearby, and after a while
the maiden arrived. She was dressed in a robe of red silk with a
collar of gold, studded with rubies and emeralds. She had the
fairest, most golden hair that Kilhuch had seen, the clearest
skin, and the rosiest cheeks. When Kilhuch saw her, he knew
that he was in love.

Kilhuch declared his love to Olwen, and she said that to win her, he would have to do whatever her father asked. So Kilhuch and his knights asked to talk with Yspathaden Penkawr, Olwen's father.

When they met him, Yspathaden lifted up his eyebrows, which had fallen right over his eyes, using a forked twig. "Now I can see the man who wants to be my son-in-law," he said, promising to tell them in the morning whether he would give his consent to the marriage. Then he picked up a poison dart from beside him and hurled it at Bedwyr. Quick as a flash, the knight caught the dart and threw it back to Yspathaden, hitting him in the knee. "So much the worse for my son-in-law," snarled Yspathaden.

Next day, when they came again to see Yspathaden, the old man said he should ask Olwen's grandparents before giving his consent. As they were leaving, Yspathaden again picked up a dart, throwing it at Menw. Like Bedwyr, Menw caught the dart and cast it back to the old man, hitting him in the back. "So much the worse for my son-in-law," he said again.

The following day Yspathaden threw a dart at Kilhuch, who caught it yet again. When Kilhuch threw the dart back, it caught Yspathaden in the eye. "So it is you who seek my daughter?" he said.

"Yes, it is I," replied Kilhuch.

"Then this is what I want you to do." And Yspathaden went on to describe a series of quests that Kilhuch was to undertake before he could win the hand of Olwen. He was to find the razor, comb, and scissors belonging to boar Truith, the only ones that would tame Yspathaden's unruly hair. He was to find the huntsman Mabon, who would help him on the quest. And he would track down Mabon's kinsman Eidoel, said to be as difficult to find as Mabon. When he had done all these things, Yspathaden would allow him to marry his daughter.

The knights spoke to Arthur about their quest, and he agreed to go with them. They soon found Eidoel imprisoned in the

castle of Glivi, who let them take his prisoner when he heard of their quest. But no one knew where they might find Mabon, although they asked every man they met. Then Gwrhyr began to talk to the birds and beasts. He searched out the Ousel of Cilgwri, one of the oldest of birds, and asked him about Mabon. "Many years have I been here," said the Ousel.

"But I have heard nothing of Mabon. But there is one family of animals that has been here longer than me. Search out the Stag of Redynvre."

When they found the Stag, he said "I have been here many years. I have seen yonder oak tree grow from a sapling and wither away to a stump. And in all that time I have heard nothing of Mabon." The Stag told them to ask the Owl of Cwm Cawlwyd, who was older still.

When they found the Owl, he said "Long have I been here. I have watched entire woodlands grow, men fell them, and new woods grow in their place. But in all that time I have not heard tell of Mabon. Seek out the Eagle of Gwern Abwy, the oldest bird of all."

So they went to find the Eagle, who told them "When first I came here, this rock was a tall cliff. Now it has worn away. But in all this time I have not heard of Mabon. Once, when I was flying above a river, I tried to catch a Salmon at Llyn Llyw. Instead, the fish caught me, and tried to pull me under the water. It was a narrow escape. That creature swims up and down the River Severn, hearing news of all men and creatures. Seek out the Salmon and tell him of your quest."

Finally they found the Salmon, who told them about his travels. "When I swim down the river to Gloucester, there I see a strong walled city with a great prison. Go there and you may find the man you seek."

So Arthur, his knights, and the birds and beasts they had met travelled to Gloucester and stood outside the prison walls. Inside they could here a terrible wailing.

"Who is within?" asked Gwrhyr.

"It is Mabon, imprisoned here," came the reply, and they knew their quest was almost at an end. Arthur stormed the prison, and then Kay and Bedwyr broke into the dungeon and rescued Mabon. It remained only for them to find the razor, comb and scissors of the boar Truith.

When they found the boar, they had to chase him all across the land of Wales. The creature and his seven young piglets made a brave stand, and Arthur's men had to kill them one by one, until only Truith remained. At last, they cornered the boar, and Mabon and Kay managed to seize his razor and scissors. But the boar would not give up his comb, until they chased him into the sea and he disappeared beneath the waves.

Kilhuch, Arthur, Mabon, Eidoel, and all the knights returned to seek Yspathaden and Olwen. Yspathaden was shaved with the razor of Truith, and then he turned to Kilhuch.

"You shall have my daughter," he said, grudgingly. "For you have won her, although you could not have done it without the help of Arthur. I give her to you, even though it grieves me to lose her."

So Kilhuch, son of King Kilyth, finally married his Olwen, and Arthur and his knights returned to their round table.

Beth Gellert

More than anything in the world, Prince Llewelyn loved to hunt. When he was ready for the chase he would stop by the castle gate and blow his hunting horn. All his hounds would come running, and fastest and keenest of all was his favorite hound, Gellert. This hound had been a gift from the prince's father-in-law, King John. The prince loved the hound because, although he was brave as a lion when hunting, he was the gentlest creature at home, and was especially fond of the prince's young son, still a babe in arms.

The dog would always come to his master's bidding and was usually the first to scent a deer and lead the huntsmen to their quarry. Few were the days when they returned home without venison for the prince's table when Llewelyn went hunting with Gellert.

One morning Llewelyn waited by the castle gatehouse and blew his horn to call his hounds as usual. All the hounds came running to the call except for Gellert. Llewelyn was surprised, for this rarely happened, so he sounded the horn once more, but still Gellert did not appear. In the end, they gave up their

wait and Llewelyn rode off
without his favorite hound.

That day they had poor
hunting. They rode far, but
the few deer they sighted
managed to escape, and
Llewelyn and his men
went home empty-handed.
The prince felt that it was
because he did not have his
best hound with him, and he
was angry when he returned
to the castle. As he
approached the gatehouse,
who should come running
towards him but his favorite
hound? At first Llewelyn was
overjoyed. But then, as the
dog grew near him, he saw
that the animal's muzzle was
dripping with blood.

The prince was mystified,
but a horrible suspicion came
to him. He thought of his

young son, just one year old, and how Gellert loved to play with the child. Could it be that the dog had harmed the child? Quickly, the prince bounded up the stairs to the nursery.

When he got to the room, his fears were confirmed. The baby's basket lay upset on the floor, and there was no sign anywhere of Llewelyn's son. He looked more closely, and there was blood on the cradle. Surely the dog had murdered his child. Frantically, the prince searched for his son, but he could only find more patches of blood and signs of a struggle. He turned to Gellert, saying, "Monster! You have killed and eaten my son." And without further ado, the prince drew his sword and plunged it into the greyhound's side. The dog howled in pain and expired, gazing, as if in wonder, at his master's face.

As Gellert howled, a small, plaintive cry came from somewhere on the other side of the room. Straight away, Llewelyn realised his fatal mistake. He strode across the room, and looked beneath the baby's basket. Sure enough, there was his baby son, unharmed, and waking from sleep. Beside the child was the body of a great wolf, its flesh torn and bloodied. Gellert had not killed the boy, but had stood guard and protected him from the wolf. The prince hung his head in regret and shame.

Llewelyn knew he could do nothing to bring his faithful hound back to life. He took Gellert's body out of the castle walls, and carried him to a spot where the peak of Snowdon could be seen. Here they made his grave, and when the hound had been buried with due ceremony, the prince piled a cairn of stones over the burial so that all would know the spot.

Ever since, the place of the hound's burial has been called Beth Gellert, the Grave of Gellert. If a passerby asks about the grave, the locals always tell this story, so that every visitor shares a little of the prince's grief for his hound. As for Llewelyn, it was a long time before he relished the hunt once more.

The Emperor's Dream

Macsen Wledig was emperor of Rome and his empire was so great that twenty kings were his subjects. He took the kings out hunting from time to time, and on one of these hunts the emperor grew tired. So his servants made a comfortable place for him and before long, Macsen Wledig was fast asleep, and dreaming.

Macsen dreamed that he was going on a long journey. He crossed fields and rivers, hills and mountains, until at last he came to a harbor. Macsen dreamed that he stepped aboard the finest ship, which was built of gold, silver, and ivory, and set sail across the ocean. He sailed until he came to a beautiful island, where there was a castle, bigger than any he had seen in his life. The castle was decorated all over with gold, and in his dream the emperor entered the building and met the people who lived there. There was an aged man, who seemed to be a king, two fine young princes, and the most beautiful maiden that Macsen had ever seen. When she saw Macsen, the maiden stood up and embraced him, and Macsen felt greater happiness than he had ever known.

It was at this point that the emperor awoke, to realise that this vision was nothing but a dream. The beauty of the maiden, her white and gold garments, the jewelery of rubies and pearls that she wore, the gold decoration of the castle, all had seemed so real—and now Macsen's heart was filled with sadness that everything had been an illusion.

The emperor returned to Rome, and nothing would rouse him from his sadness. He no longer wanted to hunt, and he neglected his duties of state. Fine food, music and dancing meant nothing to him. Eventually one of his advisers spoke quietly to Macsen, "My lord, your men are worried. They can get no answer from you about questions of state, and you no longer enjoy anything in your life."

And so it was that Macsen explained about his dream and why he was so sad. Quickly the servant called all the wise men of the empire together, and they listened to Macsen's story. One of the wise men said, "This beautiful maiden may yet live in the world. Send out your men to the four corners of the empire; they may find her and bring her to you."

So the emperor's men set out, traveling far and wide. But after a while, they began to return. None had found the fair maiden of Macsen's dream, and the emperor seemed even sadder than before.

Then another of the wise men spoke up. "My lord, I suggest that you go yourself to the place where you had your dream. Then set out from that spot and see if you can find the places that you saw when you slept." Macsen thought that this was a good idea, and he and his men set off.

When they got to the place where the emperor had rested, they looked around them, and Macsen began to look towards a distant range of mountains. "This looks like the way I saw in my dream," he said. And the emperor sent his men off in the direction that he thought he had traveled in his dream.

Far they rode, the messengers of the

emperor. They crossed fields and rivers, climbed hills and mountains, until they had made their way across France and found a fine ship of silver, gold, and ivory. "Truly, this must be the ship," they said. They spoke to the captain and set sail across the sea until they came to Britain. Here they traveled still further, retracing the steps of Macsen's dream until they came to a great castle decorated in gold. And there, within the castle, they met the old man, his two sons, and the fairest maiden they had seen. They returned at once to Rome and brought Macsen to the place. And when they arrived, they hailed the maiden, Elen, as empress of Rome, and Macsen and she were married. The emperor grew friendly with Elen's brothers, Cynan and Adeon, and their father, Eudaf, and he stayed many years in their castle. Meanwhile, the people of Rome thought that Macsen had left them for good and chose another to be their emperor.

The new emperor wanted to make sure that Macsen would

not return to claim his throne, so he sent word to Macsen that he would be killed if he should return. "How dare he take my rightful place?" said Macsen. And straight away he called his men together and left Britain for Rome.

Swiftly they rode across France and Burgundy, conquering as they went. Soon all the empire in the west was under Macsen's rule—except for Rome itself, where the new emperor held out. Macsen lay siege to the city, but the new emperor would not give in. So Macsen's army surrounded the city for a whole year, and still the emperor stood his ground. He would not surrender.

Toward the end of this year,

word came to Britain of Macsen's difficulty, and Cynan and Adeon decided to go to Rome to help him. Elen recognized them as soon as they arrived, and they came forward to greet their sister and to see how Macsen was faring.

"Truly Macsen's soldiers are brave," said Adeon to his brother, "but we have greater cunning." Cynan suggested that they attack when the rival emperors were eating dinner, when no fighting normally took place and everyone was off their guard. They had their carpenters make ladders for everyone, and then, when the food was served, the Welsh soldiers scaled the walls and took the city by surprise. Soon the gates were opened, Macsen entered Rome, and the new emperor fled in confusion. Macsen was grateful for the help given him by Cynan and Adeon and spoke to them in thanks: "Thanks to you, my empire is my own once more. Take command now of my army and conquer what lands you will."

So Cynan and Adeon marched westwards with their army, conquering fine kingdoms for themselves in Britain and Brittany while Macsen and Elen ruled in Rome. And as long as they were on the throne there was peace between Rome and the lands of the west.

King Lludd and the Plagues of Britain

One of the greatest of all kings of Britain was King Lludd. When he came to the throne as a young man he found the greatest city in his kingdom in disrepair. He ordered it to be restored with fine stones of many colors and when it was finished, he spent most of his time in his castle in his city, which became known as Caer Lludd, or Lludd's fortress, the origin of the name London.

Lludd's favorite relative was his youngest brother, Llefelys, and the two were close companions. One day, when Lludd had been king for some seven years, Llefelys came to his brother. "Brother, the king of France has a beautiful daughter. We love each other dearly and I wish to marry her."

Lludd was pleased that the two young people loved each other, and gave his consent right away. Their joy was tinged with sorrow, however, for, just before the wedding, the king of France died, and Llefelys became ruler of his new country from his wedding day onward.

All went well for another seven years. The two realms were at peace and Caer Lludd prospered as never before. Then one day came a series of misfortunes to Lludd's kingdom.

First came a wicked band of mischief-makers, a people known as the Coranieid. They seemed to get every-where, hearing all Lludd's plans and keeping one step ahead of him whenever he tried to expel them from the island. They listened in to every private conversation, and could cause ill will between friends by telling lies about what people had said.

Second was a mysterious piercing scream, which was heard every May Day. In every house in the land, this

scream could be heard, and anyone who was unlucky enough to hear its full blast suffered soon afterward. The young lost their energy and beauty, the old lost their sense, even crops and trees became diseased and died when the scream made itself heard. And yet no one in the kingdom knew where the scream came from or what creature could be making it.

The final terror of the land of Britain was a terrible famine at the king's court. Now Lludd had always been a generous king, who stocked his larders well and was hospitable to all comers. But when this plague struck, no matter how full his grain bins or how many bottles of wine or barrels of ale he kept in his storerooms, all the food and drink seemed to disappear.

Lludd was baffled about how to stop the second and third

plagues, but he supposed he could fight the wicked people who caused the first, and set sail to France, to ask his brother for help. Lludd explained his difficulty to his brother, and Llefelys produced a special bronze speaking horn, so that they could talk into each other's ears, without being overheard.

At first, they found it difficult to make themselves heard through the horn, and Llefelys said "There is a demon in this speaking horn. Bring me wine, and we will flush the demon out." Sure enough, when they poured wine down the tube, out came a tiny demon, holding his nose so as not to drown in the liquid.

Lludd first explained to his brother about the Coranieid. "Take some of these insects," said Llefelys. "Grind them up and

dissolve the pieces in water. When you have done this, call everyone in your kingdom together, both British and Coranieid. Sprinkle this water over all of them—it will kill only your enemies."

Next, Lludd told his brother about the mysterious scream. "Surely that is the sound of two dragons fighting," said Llefelys. "You must measure your kingdom and find the precise center. Here, dig a pit, fill it with gallons of your finest mead, and cover it with a great cloth. Then wait for the dragons to come. When they are tired of their fight, they will turn into two pigs, and will rest, exhausted, on the cloth. They will fall into the mead and you must bury them quickly."

Finally Lludd told his brother about the famine at court. "A great magician with unstoppable hunger and thirst is stealing your food and drink," said Llefelys. "Keep watch for him, with a tub of ice-cold water nearby. He will try to send you to sleep, so when you feel tired, jump into the water to keep yourself awake. Then you will be able to fight the magician."

Lludd thanked his brother and returned to his kingdom, where he began to do what Llefelys had advised.

Sure enough, when he sprinkled the water over everyone, only the Coranieid dropped down dead; the Britons were all hale and hearty. Next he dug his pit and killed the dragons.

Then Lludd lay in wait for the magician, jumping into the cold water when he started to feel drowsy. "Leave my meat and drink alone!" shouted Lludd, when the magician started to fill his huge basket. At once, the two men began to fight. They hit out and slashed with their swords until the weapons were blunt. They battered each other with their shields. They even fought with their fists. In the end, Lludd pinned the magician against the ground and the thief begged for mercy.

"Spare me, and I will right all the wrongs I have done you."

Lludd paused and looked at his opponent. Ever a generous man, Lludd was merciful, and the magician served him all his life. The plagues of Britain were banished, and Lludd is still remembered as a great and merciful king.

The Boy Who Went to Fairyland

Many years ago in southern Wales lived a boy called Elidor. He was a bright lad and his mother wanted him to become a priest, so she sent him to study with a good, but strict, teacher.

By the time he was twelve, Elidor was doing well in all his lessons, but he could not bear the beatings he got from his master. So one day, he ran away and hid near a river, where the waters had hollowed out a cave by its banks.

The lad stayed in his hollow for two days, and had nothing to eat while he was there. He was just about to give in and go back hungry to his teacher when he turned and found himself looking down on two tiny men. Elidor's jaw dropped and he looked silently at the two small creatures, for in truth he did not know what to do or say. Then one of the men spoke to him: "If you come with us, we will take you to a place where there is play and pleasure all day long."

Elidor thought of the hard work and harsh punishment that awaited him at home, and agreed to follow the little men. They took him deep down into the cave, which turned into a dark underground tunnel, before opening out into a landscape of rivers, fields, woodlands, and plains. This land was more beautiful than the countryside around Elidor's home, but darker, because no sun shone there. As he looked around him, Elidor's eyes got used to the dark, and he could make out woods and streams, plains and meadows, the latter growing with beautiful flowers, the like of which he had not seen before.

Elidor paused to look at the beauty around him, but the two men hurried him along. He soon realised that the men were taking him to their leader. The king, who was much taller than his subjects, sat with all his court around

him, and looked at Elidor curiously. The king's courtiers, most of whom were pale-skinned with long, flowing, shoulder-length hair, also stared at Elidor, for they had never been so close to a mortal before. Finally, when everyone had looked at him and marveled at him for some time, the king led Elidor to a young creature, who turned out to be his son.

When the fairy prince and Elidor had introduced themselves, and the prince had heard how the two little men had found Elidor near the cave, the prince turned to the young boy, "You must be hungry after all this time without food. Come with me." And they went off to a banqueting hall, where Elidor ate the first of many amazing meals. He quickly saw that the food of fairyland was unlike the fare he was used to. There was no meat or fish, and the little people normally ate foods that looked like milky puddings, made with all sorts of different fruits and flavored with spices. When he had eaten his fill, the prince told Elidor about the ways of the fairy kingdom.

The fairies, it seemed, were a gentle, peace-loving people, who came and went often between their land and the world of humans. But because the fairies were small and silent, rarely did any mortal see them or even suspect that they were there. So it was that, while humans knew little of the ways of the fairies, the little people knew a great deal about mortals—their farms and their towns, their people and kings, their beliefs and their wars.

In turn, Elidor learned much about the fairies. He found that they traveled between their world and the human world through a variety of different routes. But he could never remember the ways through their passages, so baffling were their twists and turns, and he realised now why no human being had ever found their strange world before.

The little people had no gods or churches, but they held one thing sacred above all else—the truth. They acted peacefully and honestly with each other at all times, and were rather scornful of humans, with their jealousies, arguments, and wars.

As Elidor won the trust of the little people, they allowed him

to visit his own world and return to fairyland. When he first told his mother where he had been, she did not believe him. She still listened, fascinated, to his stories of the little people and their ways. But Elidor felt she was listening in the way that a person listens to a good story, rather than one who is hearing the truth. So he wondered what he could do to convince her that what he was saying was true.

He had often told his mother that gold, although precious in the mortal world, was a commonplace metal in fairyland. He and the king's son even played games of catch with a golden ball. So Elidor decided that he would bring back the golden ball to show his mother.

Next time Elidor and the prince finished their game of

catch, Elidor stealthily picked up the golden ball. Then he made his way quietly up the dark passage into the cave and out towards the mortal world. He did not realise until too late that the little people were running after him. As he reached his mother's house, he ran faster in his excitement, tripping as he raced through the front door. The ball slipped from his hands, just as his two tiny followers burst into the room after him. The first of them scooped up the ball, then they turned on their heels and dashed off, glaring at Elidor, who realized how stupid and selfish he had been.

Immediately he ran the way he had come, intending to return and apologize to the little people. He reached the river, and found the place where the bank overhung the water. But when he entered the cave, he realised that everything had changed. There was no longer a dark passageway inside the cave. Elidor came out of the darkness, and walked up and down the river bank, thinking that he had mistaken the place. He even went back several times, in the hope that he had been mistaken and would find the passage. But try as he did, Elidor never again found the entrance to fairyland. His time with the little people was over.

Arthur's Resting Place

There was once a cattle drover who had to drive a herd of fine cattle all the way from Wales to sell them in London. He knew that he needed a good staff to carry as he walked, and to prod any cattle who wandered from the road, so he stopped by a hazel tree to cut himself a branch.

The young man drove the cattle all the way to London, found the market, and sold them for his master. He had made good time and had not visited the great city before, so he decided to rest awhile there and see some of the sights before returning to Wales. The drover stood on London Bridge admiring the view, when an old man came up to him.

"That's a fine staff you are carrying," said the old man. "I would like to see the tree that it came from, and it would be worth your while to show me."

"Then you will have to come with me all the way to Wales," answered the drover. "For that is where I cut the staff."

So, once the drover had paid for his board and lodgings, the two set off, back down the long road to Wales. When they arrived, the drover led the old man straight to the hazel tree, and the old man pointed to a narrow passage at the foot of the tree, which the drover had not noticed before.

"Come with me down this passage," said the old man. One after the other, they squeezed through the narrow opening. They walked for a few minutes and the passage began to widen. A large bell hung from the ceiling, and next to the bell was the entrance to a cave. The two men eased their way around the bell, into the cave, and what they saw next quite

took the drover's breath away.

A group of knights lay sleeping, and at their head was a noble figure, crowned and robed, who looked to the drover like a king. The glinting of their metal armor lit up the cave. "It is King Arthur and his knights," whispered the old man. "They sleep until the kingdom needs them, when Arthur will rise up and reign over a golden age."

As the old man said the words "golden age", the drover noticed something even more amazing. Next to the king were two great heaps of gold and silver. "You may take as much as you want," said the old man, "as long as you do not wake

Arthur or his men." The old man explained that if any of the knights stirred, they would ask "Is it day?" and the drover must reply "No, sleep on." Above all, the drover must not touch the great bell, which would give Arthur the warning signal to arise and kill his enemies.

The drover started to gather his first load of gold, and he was surprised to see that the old man was not taking any himself. "It is not gold and silver that makes me wise," said the old man knowingly.

The drover started as he dropped a gold coin on the floor of the cave. One of the knights stirred.

"Is it day?" groaned the knight.

"No, sleep on," said the drover. And he tiptoed out of the cave, just squeezing past the bell with his heavy load.

A second time the drover entered the cave. Again, one of the knights seemed to be waking.

"Is it day?"

"No, sleep on."

And even though his heap of coins was large and bulky, the drover managed again to get past the bell without touching it.

But the third time he entered the cave, the drover, more confident than before, was also more careless. As he was leaving, he brushed the bell, and its deep ring echoed all around. Before he could move, knights began to leap up and circle him.

The drover was surrounded by clanking armor and shouting knights. The noise, in the echoing cave, was awesome, and the drover dropped his load of gold and silver in terror, and began to run. But one of the knights caught him, and several started to give him a beating. Somewhere in the fray he heard several of the knights yelling, "Wales is in danger! The hour is come!"

But suddenly, a louder voice rang out above the others. "Enough! Lay down your arms! Would you rise from your sleep for *him*?" Then the cave was silent, for it was Arthur himself who spoke. Only a single knight, Kay, held on to the drover, and when the king glanced at

Kay, he threw his captive roughly against the hard wall of the cave. Picking himself up, the drover ran down the passage and out into the light, thinking only of escaping with his life. Behind him, he heard a loud rumbling as a great stone was pushed to seal the entrance of the cave. But the drover thought little of this as he ran home, thankful that he had escaped with a few wounds and bruises.

The drover's friends and relatives asked him how he came by his wounds, but it was a long time before he told his story. Finally, though, he described the passage, the cave, and the sleeping king to a group of friends, and they decided to arm themselves and return to see if they could recover some more gold and silver from Arthur's cave.

Together they went to the place where the hazel tree grew. But they could no longer find any tree growing there, nor was there any stone, nor any passage to the cave. The drover's friends looked suspiciously at their companion. It seemed that he had made up the whole story, and they rounded on him, calling him a fool and a liar.

They went on and on with their taunts, until the drover could stand it no more. So he left home, and since has not been seen. By now he must be long dead, and no one expects him to come back. But people still talk of the return of Arthur, who one day will wake from his slumber under the hills.

Brewery of Eggshells

A shepherd and his wife lived among the hills at Treneglwys. The shepherd won respect for his care for his sheep, which always produced fine lambs. The wife kept a tidy home and cooked good food. The two lived in happiness, and one day their joy was crowned with twins, a boy and a girl.

All went well until a messenger arrived at the shepherd's cottage. A neighbor, some distance away across the hills, was ill, and the messenger asked the woman if she would go to the aid of her friend.

The woman was unwilling to leave the babies, but finally decided that she must help her neighbor. So she tucked the infants up in their cot, and set off to see what she could do. She walked as quickly as she could, for she had heard that the little people had been seen in the neighborhood. But it was the middle of the day, and she thought it unlikely that the fairies would be about in broad daylight. Sure enough, when she returned she found her twins safe where she had left them.

Everything seemed to be well, but after a month or two, both parents sensed that there was something wrong with the twins.

Neither of them seemed to be growing at all.

The shepherd looked at his wife, and at his son and daughter. "They cannot be our children," he said.

"But they must be ours," objected his wife. "Whose else could they be?"

And so it was that the shepherd and his wife argued day and night, and their happiness seemed to be at an end. Meanwhile, the twins showed no signs of growing. The woman thought once more of the fairy people, and worried that they had interfered with her children.

The shepherd's wife had heard tell that in the town of Llanidloes there lived an old man, famous for his wisdom. She decided that she would visit him and ask his advice, both about the children and the strife between her and her husband.

She was tired when she reached Llanidloes, for the journey was long, but she went straight to the wise man's house. It would soon be harvest time and she did not want to delay. The wise man listened patiently to the woman's story, and then told her what she should do.

"It is soon harvest time and you will be making food for the reapers. Take a hen's egg and clean out the shell. Put some of the reapers' broth in the shell and take it to your door. Listen carefully to see if the twins say anything. If you hear them talking in a way that is beyond the normal understanding of children, you must take them up in your arms, carry them to Lake Elvyn, and throw them into the water. If you hear them say nothing unusual, then leave them be and do them no harm."

The woman thanked the wise man and returned home, and soon the first day of the harvest was come. The shepherd's wife made a broth to take to the reapers in the fields. She cleaned out an eggshell, filled it with broth, and took it to the door. As she listened, she heard the piping voice of one of her children recite these words:

Acorn before oak I knew,
An egg before a hen,
But I never heard of an eggshell brew
As a dinner for harvest men.

The woman looked sadly at the two children. She knew now that they were children of the little people and that she must throw them into the lake, yet she found it hard to be so cruel. But she took a deep breath and, remembering the words of the wise man, gathered the twins up in her arms and made off towards Lake Elvyn. When she got to the shore she threw them into the water. Immediately, lots of small, goblin-like creatures wearing blue trousers appeared and caught the babies.

When she returned to her house, the woman was overjoyed to see two healthy children in the cot from which she had taken the changelings. Her own children were returned, and her strife with her husband was over.

The Lost Kingdom

In former times, the best land in Wales lay towards the West. The fertile plains and lush grasslands were fine country for farming, and all who worked these fields grew rich. But there was one problem with the country in the West. The ground lay so low that it was often flooded by the sea. So the kings of the West built a great wall, with strong sluice gates, to hold back the sea. For many years the people of the West enjoyed a life without floods, and they became the envy of all Wales.

One of the greatest of all the western kings was Gwyddno. Sixteen beautiful cities grew up in his kingdom while he

reigned, and the lands of the West became more prosperous than before. After the king, the most important person in the kingdom of the West was a man called Seithennin, whom Gwyddno appointed as the keeper of the sluices. Whenever a storm brewed, and the sea threatened to overwhelm the kingdom, Seithennin would close the great sluice gates, and the lands of the West would be safe.

Seithennin was a big, strong man, chosen because he could easily turn the handles to close the heavy oak sluice gates. But there was a problem. Seithennin was a drunkard. Sometimes, when he had had too much to drink, he would be late to close the gates, and there would be some slight flooding. But the kingdom would recover, and no great harm was done.

One day, King Gwyddno ordered a great banquet in his hall. All the lords and ladies of the kingdom were there, as well as

other men of importance such as Seithennin. The banquet went on long into the night, and the sluice-keeper got more and more drunk. There was singing and harping, and everyone was enjoying themselves to the full. But because of all the noise of the reveling, no one could hear that a great storm was brewing up outside. Even when people did start to notice, they assumed that Seithennin had closed the sluice gates and that they would be safe from flooding, as they had been for years now. But no one saw that the sluice-keeper, who had drunk more than anyone else at the banquet, was fast asleep.

Outside, the waters of the sea were pouring through the sluice gates. Soon the fields were flooded and the streets of the towns were awash. But still the banquet went on, until the flood waters poured through the doors of Gwyddno's hall. There had been floods in this part of Wales in earlier years, before the sea wall was built. Then people had lost their lives and good farm land had been spoiled.

But this time it was worse. The water poured in with such speed that it was unstoppable. Men, women, and children, lords and servants alike, were swept under the flood. Even those who knew the sea, including many fishermen who were excellent swimmers, lost their lives. Sheep and cattle went the same way. Soon the whole great kingdom of the West, every field and every town, was deep under the water. And all were drowned

apart from one man, the poet Taliesin, who survived to tell the tale. They say that the sigh that Gwyddno let out as he was lost under the waves was the saddest sound ever heard.

The sea now covers Gwyddno's former kingdom, in the place now called Cardigan Bay. Occasionally, at low tide, wooden posts and fragments of stone wall are revealed among the sand, and men say that these are the last remaining parts of one of Gwyddno's cities. Sailors and fishermen who cross the bay say that they can sometimes hear the bells of the sixteen cities, sounding beneath the waves, reminding them of the terrible power of the sea. Some even say that on a quiet, still day they can hear the echoing sound of Gwyddno's final sigh.

Where Time Stood Still

The countryside in eastern Glamorgan used to be famous for sightings of the mischievous little people. They were said to use their singing to tempt people away from their path, so that many a traveler ended up in a pond or marsh; they were also well known for their habit of stealing children.

This last thing worried one woman more than most. She was a young widow, who had a small farm and a three-year-old son. She was the best of mothers, and her son was seldom out of her sight. But sometimes, she would have to leave her son indoors when she went out to check the beasts in the cow-house, and she worried that the fairies would get in while she was gone.

One day, while she was cooking, she heard a noise in the cow-house and went to investigate. When she had finished, she ran back to her house as usual. Panic filled her heart as she saw that her child had gone. She searched the house and all the farm buildings, calling "Rhoddri! Rhoddri!" But nowhere could she find the boy.

It began to grow dark, and the widow, despairing at ever

finding her child, sat down in her kitchen and wept. Suddenly
she heard a noise, and looked up to see a small figure standing
by the door. "Mother," it said.

The widow looked at the child curiously. He did not look at
all like Rhoddri. "You cannot be my Rhoddri," she said.

"Yes, it's me," replied the child.

Confused, she ushered the child into the room and gave it
food. The boy was thankful for his food, and seemed to behave
like Rhoddri used to. So the little child stayed with the widow,
and she looked after him just as carefully as she had looked
after Rhoddri. And yet a mother knows her children, and the
woman could not believe that it was he.

As the months went on, the boy did not seem to grow as her true son had done. The widow was convinced he was a changeling, left by fairies who had taken Rhoddri. She decided to consult a wise man, to see if she could find the truth.

The wise man listened carefully to the woman's story, and gave her the recipe for a brew. She should make this brew and put some of it into half an eggshell, and listen to what the child said as she did this.

When the widow got home, she lost no time, and was soon pouring the brew into the eggshell. She heard the child speaking: "Great oaks from little acorns grow. I saw the acorn long ago." And as he recited the lines he looked uglier and more annoyed than ever before.

The widow returned to the wise man to ask the meaning of the child's words. "He is saying that he remembers the acorn before it was an oak tree," said the wise man. "He is an ancient infant and truly one of the little people. To get back your own

child you will have to do two more things, and I shall now tell
you the first. In three days' time it will be full moon. Go to the
crossroads at midnight, hide yourself and wait. You may see
something which will make you cry, but keep quiet. If you
make any noise, you will lose your child for ever. Then return
to me and tell me what you have seen."

Trembling with fear, the widow made her way to the crossroads on the evening of full moon. There was a thorn bush
nearby, so she hid herself behind and waited. After a while she
heard music and voices, and as the music got nearer, she felt
more and more sleepy. But she fought to keep herself awake,
and through the leaves she saw a group of little people, the
men with red hats, the women with blue and green skirts,
dancing along and singing. Amongst them was Rhoddri, and
the fairies seemed to be guarding the boy. At once, she felt a
cry welling up inside her, but, remembering the words of the
wise man, she stifled the cry, let the fairy procession pass,

and returned to her cottage. Her relief at seeing her child alive and well was tainted with sadness because she had let him go, but she trusted the wise man.

"It is as I thought," said the wise man, when the widow told the story of the fairy procession. Then he told her the second thing she should do. "Find a black hen and kill her, but do not pluck her feathers. Let the changeling see what you are doing, but do not make any remark to him. Next close all your doors and windows, and roast the hen. Then, as the feathers fall from the roasting fowl, watch the fairy child carefully."

The widow left the wise man and went to carry out his bidding. There was no black hen among the widow's own fowls, so she called on each of her neighbors.

At the last house in the village she met a woman carrying a sieve. "I can't carry any sunlight into my house using this sieve," said the woman. "I don't know what to do."

"Why, open your shutters," replied the widow. "That will bring the sun into your house."

The woman saw that this was good advice, and happily gave the widow a black hen in thanks. So the widow took the hen, and roasted it as she had been told. As the feathers began to fall from the bird, she heard music playing outside her house. She concentrated on what she was doing, and watched the feathers falling off the hen. As the last feather fell, there was a loud blast of music outside. She looked around and the fairy child had vanished. Now she had no child at all. She sat in despair, looking at the remains of the roast fowl, and wondering what to do next. Suddenly, she heard a cry coming from outside the house. She rushed out, saw her own lost Rhoddri, and swept him into her arms.

The child seemed mystified at his mother's joy, especially when she asked him where he had been for the past year.

"But I have not been away a year," said the child. "I only stayed a few minutes, to listen to the music."

The Cry of Vengeance

Long ago in the ancient town of Bala lived a wicked prince called Tegid Foel. All his people feared him, for if anyone got in his way, or disagreed with him, the prince had them killed.

Some men plotted to dethrone the prince, but none of them succeeded, for Tegid Foel surrounded himself with guards and henchmen who were almost as ruthless as himself. One day, the prince heard a small voice, whispering in his ear, "Vengeance will come, vengeance will come!" Tegid took no

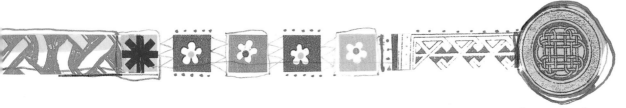

notice of the voice, even though he heard it again, and soon he heard it every day. And the prince's rule carried on for many years of cruelty, until his three sons were grown up and his first son was married.

Tegid Foel's castle was usually a quiet, somber place, but one day there was noise of rejoicing there. The wife of Tegid's first son had given birth to her first child, a grandson for the prince, and a great feast was ordered. Everyone in the kingdom was invited—and woe betide anyone who did not attend.

One of those who did not want to come was a young, peace-loving harper from the hills near Bala. He was known as the best musician for miles around, and Tegid wanted him to play at his feast. The harper knew that there would be trouble if he did not go, so he took his harp and strode to the castle.

When the harper arrived, the banquet was already beginning, so he took his place as quickly as he could and began to tune his instrument. When the prince saw him, he roared "Waste no time! Play, harper!" in a voice that sent a chill through all who heard. So the harper sang and played, to the delight of everyone in the hall. It seemed as if his music had brought some tranquillity and beauty to the place, where the atmosphere was usually brooding and evil.

At around midnight, there was an interval, and the harper strolled outside in the courtyard to relax for a while. As he did so, a voice whispered in his ear, "Vengeance has come, vengeance has come." Then he saw a small bird that seemed to be beckoning to him with its beak. The creature seemed to be telling him to leave the castle.

At first, the harper was doubtful, and he wondered what would become of him if he left the banquet now. But he had always listened to the sounds of nature, so he decided to obey the call, slipping through the castle gates and making for the hills. When he had walked for a while, the harper paused. He realized in horror that he had left his harp behind him in the hall. At once he was in turmoil. His harp was his livelihood. But the guards had probably already noticed that he had gone. If he returned – either to play or to take the harp – he risked losing his head. So he decided to continue on his way.

Far the harper climbed into the hills, leaving the sounds of reveling behind him, until he began to tire and could walk no more. He felt that he was far enough away to be out of reach of the castle guards, who were anyway too intent on reveling to chase him tonight. So he lay down and fell asleep.

At dawn, the harper awoke and stretched and rubbed his eyes. As he looked down to the valley he saw an astounding sight. The town and castle of Bala were no more. In their place was a gigantic lake. The only sign of the previous night's feast was his harp, floating unharmed. As the ripples of the water brought the instrument back to him, the harper sighed with relief that he had listened to the quiet, sweet voice of the bird instead of the harsh, ugly voice of the prince's command.

A Rare Quarry

Two friends were out hunting otters and they walked beside a stream, looking at the banks for holes where the creatures might be hiding. Suddenly, one of them saw a flash of red. The creature moved quickly, darting along the bank and vanishing into a hole near a tree.

One friend turned to the other: "What was that? It was too large for a squirrel, too small for a fox. Could it be a rare, red-furred otter?"

The two men had never seen such an otter before, but could not think what other sort of creature it might be, so decided to try to catch it. They looked carefully at the burrow and saw that it had two entrances, one on either side of the tree. "We'll need a sack," said the first man, and he ran off to a nearby farm to borrow one.

When he returned, he held the sack over one end of the burrow, while his friend stood at the other end and made a noise to frighten the creature out. Sure enough, there was a mighty plop as the creature jumped into the sack. Holding the end closed, the two men made off for home, very pleased with their rare quarry.

The pair walked home across the fields, and had not gone very far when they were amazed to hear a tiny voice inside the sack calling "I hear my mother calling me. I hear my mother calling me." The men dropped the sack in astonishment and watched as a tiny figure climbed out. On his head was a red hat, and he wore trousers and jacket and shoes that were also bright red. As he ran off towards the cover of some low bushes, again he looked like a streak of red, and the men saw how easy it had been to mistake him for an animal.

Looking at each other in alarm, the two hunters ran off towards home. They never hunted for otters again on that stretch of the river.

The Farmer and the Goat Girl

There was once a farmer called Cadwalader. Unlike all his neighbors, who were sheep farmers, Cadwalader had a large flock of goats. Of all his goats he had a special favorite that he called Jenny, and Jenny was the whitest and most beautiful of all his flock.

For many years Jenny was Cadwalader's best milk-producer, and she was always obedient, unlike some of the stubborn

creatures in his flock. Then, one day, Jenny bolted from the field and ran away. Up the nearest mountain she went, and seemed not to be stopping, so Cadwalader gave chase.

They climbed higher and higher, Jenny always slightly ahead. When it seemed as if the farmer would catch her, she jumped on to a nearby crag, leaving Cadwalader stranded.

162

Not only did the farmer feel stupid, stuck on the mountain like this, he also collected bruises and sprains as he clambered among the rocks. Finally, he had had enough, and he picked up a stone and hurled it at the goat in frustration as she was jumping another chasm.

The stone hit Jenny in the side, and, bleating loudly, she fell far down into the gap between the rocks. Straightaway Cadwalader was full of remorse. It was only in a moment of frustration that he had wanted to hurt the animal, and now his only wish was to see that she was still alive. He clambered down to the rocky gap where she lay, and saw that, although she was still breathing, she was badly injured. He did his best to make her comfortable, and tears of sadness formed in his eyes as he saw how she was hurt.

It was now dark, but the moon appeared between the rocks and shed its light on the scene. As the moon rose, the goat turned into a beautiful young woman who was lying there before Cadwalader. He looked in bafflement at her brown eyes and soft hair, and found that not only was she beautiful, she was also well and looked pleased to see him. "So, my dear Cadwalader," she said. "At long last I can speak to you."

Cadwalader did not know what to make of all this. When the young woman spoke, there seemed to be a bleat in her voice; when she held his hand, it felt like a hoof. Was she goat or girl, or some strange mixture of the two?

As she led him towards an outcrop of rock, Cadwalader felt he was heading into danger. As they rounded a corner, they found themselves surrounded by a flock of goats—not the tame creatures Cadwalader was used to, but large wild goats,

many of which had long horns and beards. Jenny led him to the largest goat of all, and bowed, as if he were a king.

"Is this the man you want?" the goat asked Jenny.

"Yes, he is the one."

"Not a very fine specimen," said the goat-king. "I had hoped for something better"

"He will be better afterward," replied Jenny.

Cadwalader wondered what was going to happen, and looked around him in fear. Then the goat-king turned to Cadwalader.

"Will you, Cadwalader, take this she-goat to be your wife?"

"No, my lord. I want nothing to do with goats ever again." And with that, Cadwalader turned and ran for his life. He was fast, but not fast enough for the great goat-king. Coming up behind Cadwalader, the huge billy goat gave the farmer such a tremendous butt that Cadwalader fell headlong down the crag, rolling and falling, falling and rolling, until he came to a stop, unconscious, right at the bottom of the mountain.

There Cadwalader lay for the rest of the night, until he woke, aching from head to toe, at dawn. He limped home to his farm, where his goats bleated in welcome. But Cadwalader wanted to be a goat farmer no more. He drove his goats to market, and bought a flock of sheep, just like his neighbors.

Jack and his Golden Snuff-Box

Long ago in the forests of Wales few people traveled very far.
They grew their own food, built their houses and made their
furniture from timber from the forests, and kept a few sheep or
goats to provide milk and wool. So it was that there was once
a couple, getting on in years, who never left the forest. They
never saw any other people than their young son, Jack, and
were happy with their own company.

They told Jack many old stories—about kings and princes,
towns and villages—and Jack became curious to see the world
beyond the forest. One day, when his father was out cutting
wood, Jack turned to his mother. "Here I see nothing but
trees, and the only difference is the changing seasons. Let me
go away for a while and see the world, for I think I shall go
mad with boredom if I stay here."

His mother paused, for she was sad to see him go. "Well, if
you must, you must," she said. "And God go with you. But stay
awhile before you go and I will bake you a cake. Would you
like a small cake, with my blessings, or a large cake, with my
curses?"

"I am going far and may be hungry. Bake me a large cake," replied Jack.

So Jack's mother baked him a large cake, and when he left, she went to the top of the house, and cursed her son as long as she could see him.

Soon Jack met his father, who asked him where he was going. Like his mother, Jack's father was sorry to see him go, but realized that it was what the boy wanted. The old man took from his pocket a small golden box and handed it to Jack. "Take this snuff-box, keep it in your pocket, and be sure not to open it until your death is near," said the father.

Jack tramped on for many miles. By the end of the long day he had finished his cake and was still hungry. He saw a large house, so he stopped there, and asked one of the maids if there was somewhere he could stay the night. In the kitchen, the servants gave Jack some food to eat and sat him down by the fire, and soon the daughter of the house came to have a look at the young visitor.

When Jack saw the young woman, he was stunned by her beauty, and the young woman was hardly less pleased with the sight of Jack. Before long, she had called her father to see him, and the master of the house asked Jack what he could do. Jack was so fascinated by the beauty of the man's daughter that he did not think before answering, "Why, I can do anything you like."

"If you can do anything, make me a great lake in front of my house, with a fleet of sailing ships. I want one of the ships to fire a salute, and the last round of the salute must break the leg of the bed where my daughter sleeps. If you can't achieve this, then prepare to meet your doom."

Jack went to bed in gloom. He knelt down to say his prayers, thinking that he would soon be dead. And that thought

brought to mind the golden snuff-box, which he should only open when death was near. Jack took out the box and lifted the lid. Out jumped three tiny men, all dressed in red, and one of them spoke to Jack: "What do you want us to do?"

Jack explained what had been asked of him, and the little man told him to go to sleep. Much later, Jack was woken by a loud banging. When he looked through the window he saw a great lake in front of the house, on which were sailing stately men-of-war. One of these was firing a salute.

When he went down to meet the master of the house, Jack felt proud that the little men in the snuff-box had done so much for him. He felt that now he really could do anything

that was asked of him. Over breakfast, he talked with the master, who asked him to perform two more magical feats. If Jack could do these, he would be rewarded with the hand of the daughter of the house.

First of all, Jack had to fell all the tall trees within several miles of the house; this was done, and the gentleman was pleased. Jack's second task seemed even more difficult. The gentleman asked for a huge castle standing on twelve golden pillars, guarded by regiments of soldiers. With the help of the little men in his box, Jack produced the castle and the soldiers. Then the gentleman placed his daughter's hand in Jack's, and the couple looked at each other lovingly. It seemed that Jack's troubles were over. But they were only just beginning.

Jack lived happily with the gentleman and his family. He now had fine clothes and servants to do his bidding. One day, they were going out hunting. Jack's manservant, tidying his master's clothes when Jack was out on the hunt, came across the golden snuff-box. The valet opened the box in curiosity, and nearly dropped it when the three small men popped out. "What do you want us to do?" asked the men. The valet saw his chance. "I want this castle to be moved far across the sea, and I want to go with it and become its lord."

There was confusion and turmoil when Jack and the others came back from the hunt. His father-in-law rounded on Jack, accusing him of sorcery. Jack stood in misery, wondering what he could do now both castle and snuff-box were gone. "Give me a year and a day," Jack pleaded. "I will travel the world and try to find your castle."

So Jack began his travels once more. Everywhere he went he asked people about the castle, but no one could tell him where it was. When it seemed that he had asked everyone he could, he sat down in despair.

As he sat, Jack saw a little mouse looking up at him. "I don't suppose you know where the castle could be?" said Jack, half jokingly. "I guard the palace of the king of the mice," said the little creature. "Let us ask him if he knows." So to his surprise, Jack found himself in front of the mouse-king.

The king of the mice called all the mice in his kingdom to his palace, and asked all of them if they had seen the fine castle with its twelve golden pillars. None knew of its whereabouts, but one mouse suggested, "Two creatures who travel far are the king of the frogs and the king of the birds. Go and see them, and they may have news for you."

Taking with him the little mouse he had first met, Jack went off to seek these two creatures. After a long walk, they found the place where the king of the frogs lived. A frog stood guard, and at first would not let them in, but Jack insisted that he must see the king, and soon the king of the frogs came out to

ask him what he wanted. The frog-king listened to Jack's story in silence, then made an enormous and extraordinary croak, the like of which Jack had never heard before. Gradually, the land and water all around them filled with frogs, as all the king's subjects came to his call. The king asked them if they had seen the castle with twelve golden pillars, and they all croaked "No".

Jack began his journey once more. This time, he took with him the frog who had stood guard, as well as the mouse. Together, they went to search for the ruler of the birds.

Again, Jack asked to meet the king, and again was admitted. The king called all the fowls of the air around him and asked if any had seen the castle with the twelve golden pillars. Although they had flown far and wide, none of the birds had seen the castle. Jack was downhearted. It seemed that his last hope had been dashed. Then the king spoke up. "Where is the great bird?" All the feathered creatures looked about them, and it became clear to Jack that one of their number was missing.

As they waited, there was a great whooshing of wings, and an eagle appeared in the sky above their heads. The king turned

to the eagle, and asked again about the castle. "Yes, I have seen it," said the eagle. "I will take Jack to its resting place."

Jack, the mouse, and the frog clambered aboard the eagle's back and they flew to where the castle stood. Jack was puzzled about how to move the castle, but he told the mouse about his snuff-box. When they landed, the little animal ran off in search of the box, and the others hid quietly on the battlements. Soon the mouse returned, clutching the box in its paws, and they all flew off again, to make their way back to the home of Jack's father-in-law. As they flew, the mouse and the frog argued about who had been most helpful in finding the box, and, in the squabble, the box slipped into the sea below.

Jack started to panic and curse the creatures, but the eagle swooped low over the sea, and the frog dived to look for the box. Twice the frog dived and came up with nothing. The third time the frog seemed to be under the water for hours. In the end he came up, grasping the box and croaking with glee.

And so it was that the four friends returned to the land of Jack's father-in-law. Jack opened his box, out stepped the tiny men, and the castle was returned to its rightful place. The father-in-law thanked Jack, and Jack's young wife was pleased and relieved to see her husband home again. By now, she had a fine young son, all the family lived happily, and the castle with the twelve golden pillars never moved again.

The Green Man of No Man's Land

Jack was a miller and a great gambler. One day, a gentleman was passing Jack's mill and stopped to talk. The two soon began to play cards and as the game went on the stakes got higher and Jack was winning as usual—no one seemed able to beat him. Then the stranger said, "What do you want to win next."

"I will have the great castle over the way," replied Jack, and they dealt the cards.

Sure enough, Jack won again. But when they dealt again, the gentleman was the winner. "Now you must find *my* castle," said the gentleman to Jack. "My name is the Green Man of No Man's Land. I'll give you a year and a day to find my castle. If you fail, I will cut off your head."

Jack set off on horseback, for he thought that his journey would be long. He traveled far until he came to a land where it was cold and the ground was covered in snow. Jack felt cold and hungry, and decided to stop at the next house he could find.

The next house was the cottage of an old woman, who asked

Jack to come to her fireside and offered him food. Straight away, Jack asked her about the castle of the Green Man. "I do not know it," said the old woman. "But I can ask one quarter of the world if they know."

Next morning, Jack was amazed to see the old woman climb up on to the roof of her house. She raised a horn to her lips and blew a tremendous blast, and soon people came running towards her house from all directions. Surely, thought Jack, some of these people would know the Green Man's castle.

But when the old woman asked them, they all shook their heads. None of them had heard of the castle of the Green Man of No Man's Land. So the old woman blew her horn once

more, and all the birds of the neighbourhood flew to her call. She asked the birds, who had traveled far and wide in their flight. But none even of these had heard of the castle. The old woman turned to Jack.

"I have a sister further along this road. Take my horse and ride to her house. She may have heard of the Green Man's castle." And she gave Jack a ball of thread, which he was to leave trailing behind him as he rode.

Jack took the old woman's horse and rode away. When he came to the sister's house, she recognized the beast. "It is long since I have seen my sister's horse," she said. "What is your business with me?" Jack asked her about the castle of the Green Man. "I do not know it," said the sister. "But I can ask one half of the world if they know."

Next morning, Jack saw the woman climb up to the roof of her house with a horn, just as her sister had done. When she blew, an even greater crowd gathered around her house. Surely, thought Jack, some of these people would know the Green Man's castle. But once more, when the sister asked them, they all shook their heads. None of them had heard of the castle of the Green Man of No Man's Land. A second blast of the horn brought huge flocks of birds to the sky above the sister's house. But none of these had heard of the castle either.

Jack and the sister went back into the house. "I have another sister," she said. "If she does not know of this castle that you seek, then no other will know. Take my horse, and this ball of thread, and make your way to where she lives."

So Jack set off once again, trailing his thread behind him, until he came to the house of the eldest of the sisters.

At once the old woman recognized her sister's horse. Jack questioned her about the castle, but again the woman knew nothing of it. So Jack was not surprised when in the morning she blew her horn to bring still greater crowds to her house. Still no one knew, and when the woman summoned the birds, it seemed as if once more they had failed to find the castle. Then there was a whirring of wings in the sky and one last

bird, a noble eagle, appeared above their heads. "Where have you been all this long while?" asked the woman.

"I have been in the country of the Green Man of No Man's Land," said the eagle. And he told them where it was.

The eagle and the old woman told Jack to go to a place where there was a lake with three white swans. Jack was to hide by the shore until the swans came near him and shook out some of their feathers. Jack was to take these feathers and wait. "When one of the swans comes to ask for her feathers, do not give them back, but ask her to ferry you across the lake to her father's castle."

Jack set off, and did as he had been told. Sure enough, one of the swans came to Jack and asked him to return her feathers. At first, she refused to carry Jack over the lake, but Jack insisted. Then the swan said to Jack: "Very well, get up on my back. But do not tell my father that I helped you."

This was how Jack finally reached the castle of the Green Man of No Man's Land. "One of my daughters must have helped you to get here," said the Green Man.

"No," replied Jack. "I have not seen her."

"Then you must clean out my stables. And if you do not, I will cut off your head."

Jack saw no escape, so went to work. It soon became clear that the task was never ending. Every shovelful he cleared,

three more seemed to appear in its place. Then the youngest daughter appeared and offered Jack some food. While he was eating, the stable was miraculously cleared. Every bit of the filth had disappeared. Jack looked at the girl in gratitude, but she warned him: "Do not tell my father that I helped you."

When the Green Man saw the work done, he looked at Jack suspiciously. "One of my daughters must have helped you," he said.

"No," replied Jack. "I have not seen her."

"Then you must fell all the trees in my forest," said the Green Man.

Jack set to work, but the job seemed endless, with new trees springing up as soon as he cut one down. The second daughter appeared, and gave Jack some food. When Jack returned to his

task, all the trees were cut down. Again the girl warned Jack not to tell her father.

When the Green Man saw the work done, he looked at Jack once more. "One of my daughters must have helped you," he said. Jack denied that he had seen her.

"Then you must build me a new barn, and thatch it with birds' feathers."

Jack saw that this was another impossible task, and that again he would need the help of one of the daughters. Sure enough, the girl appeared and the job was completed.

Jack's next task was to collect an egg from a mountain by the lake. Before long, one of the daughters appeared and told Jack to take off his shoe. Before his eyes, it turned into

a boat, so that they could row across and pick up the egg. As they returned, the girl spoke to Jack: "Tomorrow my father will turn me and my two sisters into swans. Only the one that you choose will be saved. But if you choose all three, we will all escape."

The Green Man and Jack stood by the castle as the three swans flew overhead.

"Which one will you have," asked the Green Man. Jack chose the first of the three. Again the swans flew past, and this time Jack pointed to the second. The birds circled and passed once more, and finally Jack chose the third.

"Then she shall be your wife," said the Green Man. And so she and Jack were married, and lived happily, but the sisters were saved too. And as for the Green Man, he died soon afterwards, and he and his tricks were never heard of again.

Taliesin

Long ago in the middle of Lake Tegid lived a gentleman called Tegid Voel and his wife Caridwen. They had a daughter named Creirwy, and two sons, Morvran ab Tegid and Avagddu. The youngest child, Avagddu, was an ugly infant, and Caridwen feared that no one of noble birth would have anything to do with him. So she decided to brew him a magic potion that would give him the gifts of knowledge and shape-changing, so that he could make a better way in the world.

She added marvellous herbs and spices to her cauldron and set the mixture over the fire. To work properly, the brew had to boil for a year and a day, so Caridwen asked a young lad called Gwion to stir the cauldron, and a blind man called Morda to look after the fire.

Each day Caridwen added fresh herbs and recited spells over the pot, and the time grew near when the brew would be ready. As he was stirring, a few drops of the mixture splashed on to Gwion's finger. Automatically, Gwion licked his finger to make it clean, and straight away the young lad was blessed with the gift of seeing into the future and the ability to change his

shape into whatever he liked.
As he looked into the future,
he saw that Caridwen
planned to kill him, so
straightaway he took to his
feet and ran, knocking the
cauldron, which split in two
behind him.

Caridwen turned to Morda
and cursed him, but the blind
man pointed out that all was
Gwion's fault, and the
woman saw that she must
chase the lad and stop him.
Off she ran, and as he saw
her, Gwion changed himself
into a hare. But Caridwen
transformed herself into a
greyhound, and started to
gain on him. Next Gwion
turned himself into a fish,
leaping into the river. But
Caridwen transformed herself
into an otter, and swam after

him. Gwion left the water behind, taking the shape of a bird. But Caridwen transformed herself into a hawk and flew up after him. Gwion landed on a heap of wheat and turned himself into one of the grains. But Caridwen transformed herself into a great black hen, and pecked away at all the grains until she had swallowed him.

Gwion stayed for nine months in Caridwen's belly, and then she fell into labor and gave birth to him, and he had once more the form of a baby. When she saw her child, Caridwen could not bear to kill him. So she put him in a leather bag, and threw him into the sea.

The place where Caridwen threw Gwion into the sea was

near the weir of Gwyddno. Here Gwyddno and his ill-favored son Elphin often came to catch salmon, and it chanced that Elphin came to do just that, the day after Gwion had been abandoned.

Elphin found no fish at the weir, and was anxious that his father would be cross with him for returning empty-handed. But he found the leather bag, opened it, and was struck by the child's beauty. "Behold a radiant brow!" he said. "Let him be called Taliesin." And he set off to take the child to his father.

As they went, Taliesin startled Elphin by beginning to sing. He sang to Elphin that he should not despair, for good fortune would come to him. The song seemed to be consoling Elphin for returning home without any fish, and the man's mood began to improve. He looked at the child and asked him whether he was a human or a spirit. In reply, Taliesin sang another song, describing how he could change his shape, and how he had to change his shape to escape the clutches of Caridwen. As he sang, he embroidered his tale, imagining all the creatures he could have become:

> I have fled as a roe in a tangled thicket;
> I have fled as a wolf cub, and lived in the wilderness;
> I have fled as a thrush and sung of the future;
> I have fled as a fox, and lived by my cunning;
> I have fled as an iron in the glowing fire;
> I have fled as a spear-head, and woe to my enemies;

I have fled as a fierce bull bitterly fighting;
I have fled as white grain of pure wheat.
Into a dark leathern bag I was thrown;
On a boundless sea I was sent adrift;
And the Lord God then gave me my liberty.

When Taliesin's song was finished, they arrived at Gwyddno's court, and Elphin said, "I have something here that is better than fish—a bard."

"What use is a bard?" complained Gwyddno. But when he heard Taliesin sing, he thought that a bard might be more use than he had first believed. So he told Elphin to give Taliesin to his wife, and the woman brought up the child as lovingly as if he were her own.

Taliesin indeed seemed to bring good fortune to Elphin. Everything he did brought him either riches or favor with the king. And so it went on until Taliesin was just thirteen, when Elphin was invited to spend Christmas with his uncle, Maelgwyn Gwynedd, with all Maelgwyn's knights and squires at his castle of Dyganwy.

As knights did when they were assembled in their lord's house, the men all fell to praising Maelgwyn—his generosity, his bravery, the beauty of his queen, his fine horses, and the skill and wisdom of his bards. For bards were highly valued at this time, as they always have been in Wales, and Maelgwyn had some twenty-four bards, all skilled in poetry and music, and valuable to their lord because they could speak many languages and act as envoys and messengers for Maelgwyn.

When they had finished praising Maelgwyn and his bards, Elphin spoke up: "Far be it from me to vie with a king, but if Maelgwyn were not a king, I would say that my own wife is more beautiful and virtuous than his queen and that my bard Taliesin is more skilled than any of his bards."

Maelgwyn was full of anger at his nephew's boastfulness. "Better than the bards of the royal court?" he roared. "Clap him in irons and lock him in prison." And so Elphin found himself bundled off and locked in the castle dungeon.

When Elphin was locked away, Maelgwyn turned to his son Rhun, the most evil and graceless character in the whole court. He told Rhun to visit Elphin's wife and find out if she was indeed virtuous. The women of the court feared for Elphin's wife when they heard that Rhun proposed to call on her in her chamber.

Meanwhile Taliesin sped to Elphin's wife. "Madam, you are in danger," he said. "Change places with one of the kitchen maids. Dress her in your clothes, and give her your rings to wear." Elphin's wife did as the bard advised, and soon it was as if the maid was the noblewoman, and the noblewoman was the maid.

Sure enough, Rhun soon came to call upon Elphin's wife, and found the maid in her place. The maid invited Rhun to eat and drink, and the evil lord dropped a sleeping draught into her drink. He pulled at Elphin's ring, which the maid wore on her finger, but it would not come off. So he took his knife and cut away the finger, and returned to the king with the evidence that he had been with Elphin's wife.

Maelgwyn showed Elphin the ring, and told him that it proved his wife was lacking in virtue to let Rhun come close. But Elphin defended his wife stoutly. "My lord, I cannot deny

that this is my ring. But the finger with it never belonged to my wife, and I will tell you three reasons why. First, my wife's fingers are much more slender than this—the ring would have come off easily; second, my wife trims her nails often and carefully, whereas the nail on this finger is untrimmed; third, the hand from which this finger came has recently been kneading dough—see the traces here—and my wife has never kneaded dough since we have been married."

The king was not used to being challenged in this way, and grew mightily angry with Elphin. "Take him back to prison," roared the king. "He shall stay there until the wisdom of his

bard is also proved."

Taliesin consoled Elphin's wife. "I will free your lord from prison. I will silence the royal bards and the king will hear how I can sing." And with that, off he went to the king's hall.

Taliesin entered the hall quietly and sat in a corner where no one noticed him. As each of Maelgwyn's bards came in, Taliesin pursed his lips and made the noise "Blerm, blerm" at them as they passed. They took little notice of this until the first two bards rose to sing to the king. When they opened their lips all that would come out was "Blerm, blerm". The king thought they were drunk, and sent a servingman to tell them off, but when the bards began again, still all they could sing was "Blerm, blerm". This went on until one of the king's squires took a broom and dealt a great blow on the head to Heinin Vardd, the king's chief bard.

Heinin kneeled before the king. "Your majesty," he said. "We do not wish to mock you. The noise that comes from our mouths was put there by some spirit that lives in that youth sitting in the corner." And Heinin pointed accusingly at Taliesin. The king called Taliesin and ordered the young bard to give an account of himself, which he did in the most extra-ordinary song he had sung:

> Chief bard of Elphin am I;
> I come from the region of the summer stars;
> And every king will call me Taliesin.
> I was with my Lord in highest heaven,
> And was there when Lucifer fell from grace;
> I fought with the great Alexander,
> And know the names of all the stars;
> I was in Canaan when Absalom was slain;
> I was in the court of Don before the birth of Gwdion;
> I was instructor to Eli and Enoch;
> I was at the place of crucifixion of the merciful Son of God;
> I am a wonder whose origin no man knows.

And so the song went on, with the most beguiling of music, and the king and all his court were speechless.

When he heard that this was Elphin's bard, the king challenged his own singers to produce a better song. But as each of the king's twenty-four bards came up to the high table, still the only sound he could make was the "Blerm, blerm" noise that Taliesin had put on his lips. Then Taliesin sang again, claiming that the power of his voice would release his master Elphin from prison and that his words would tell of the virtue and beauty of Elphin's queen. The young bard's song got louder and louder, until it seemed to merge with the sound of a mighty wind that was howling around the castle battlements.

As the wind grew, Maelgwyn and his people began to be afraid that the very castle might blow down. So the king ordered Elphin to be brought from the dungeon. When the guards brought Elphin into the hall, Taliesin started to sing once more, and at his very first notes, the chain binding Elphin snapped and the young man stood free. Then the king called for Elphin's wife, and everyone could see that she still had all of her fingers. Truly she had both beauty and virtue.

Taliesin had one last trick for the cruel king. He told Elphin to bet that his horse could beat any of the king's horses in a race. Taliesin gave the youth who rode Elphin's horse twenty-four sprigs of holly, and the youth struck each of Maelgwyn's steeds with a holly sprig as he passed. Finally, when his own horse stumbled, the youth threw down his cap at the spot—but he still won the race.

After the challenge was over, Taliesin led his lord to the place where the rider had thrown down his cap. "Dig a hole here, and you will find a cauldron full of gold," declared Taliesin. It is a reward for rescuing me from the sea and taking me into your protection."

Elphin found the gold, and they all returned to the hall. The whole court listened to Taliesin's songs all night through. And though Taliesin cured the other bards so that they could sing again, none in Wales ever heard song as sweet as Taliesin sung that night.

The Sprightly Tailor

Long ago, in a castle called Sandell, lived a laird called the great MacDonald. MacDonald liked his comfort, and favoured garments called trews, which were a combination of vest and trousers in one piece. One day the laird needed some new trews, and called for the local tailor.

When the tailor arrived the great MacDonald told him what he wanted. "I'll pay you extra," promised the laird, "if you will make the trews in the church by night." For MacDonald had heard that the church was haunted by a fearful monster, and he

wanted to see how the tailor fared when faced with this beast.

The tailor had also heard stories about the monster. But he was a sprightly fellow who liked a challenge—especially if it was going to lead to some extra money. So that very night he walked up the glen, through the churchyard gate, and into

the dark church. Finding a
tombstone where he could sit,
he got to work on the trews,
and very soon the garment was
taking shape.

After a while, the tailor felt
the floor of the church begin
to shake beneath him. A hole
seemed to open up in the
stone floor and a large and
gruesome head appeared. "Do
you see this great head of mine?" a voice boomed.

"I see that, but I'll sew these," replied the tailor, holding up
the trews.

The head paused as the tailor was speaking, then began to
rise again, revealing a thick, muscular neck. "Do you see this
great neck of mine?" the monster asked.

"I see that, but I'll sew these," replied the tailor.

Next the creature's shoulders and trunk came into view. "Do
you see this great chest of mine?"

"I see that, but I'll sew these," said the tailor. And he carried
on sewing, although, to tell the truth, some of the stitches were
a little less neat than normal.

Now the beast was rising quickly, and the tailor could make

out its arms. Its voice echoed in the stone building: "Do you see these great arms of mine?"

"I see those, but I'll sew these," replied the tailor. He gritted his teeth and carried on with his work as before, for he wanted to finish by daybreak and claim his payment from the great MacDonald.

The tailor's needle was flying now, as the monster gave a great grunt and lifted his first leg out of the ground. "Do you see this great leg of mine?" he said, his voice getting even louder.

"I see that, but I'll sew these," replied the tailor, making his final stitches a little longer, so that he could finish his work before the monster could climb out of his hole.

As the creature began to raise its other leg, the tailor blew out his candle, gathered up his things, and bundled the completed trews under one arm. He made for the door as the monster was emerging, and the tailor could hear the creature's footsteps echoing on the stone floor as he ran out into the open air.

Now the tailor could see the glen stretching in front of him, and he ran for his life, faster than he had ever ran before, for all that he was a nimble man. The monster roared at him to stop, but the tailor hurried on, his feet hardly touching the ground, and finally the great MacDonald's castle loomed up ahead of him and the tailor knew he had a chance to reach its gates.

Quickly the gates opened, and quickly they closed behind the tailor – and not a moment too soon, for as the great wooden gates slammed shut, the monster crashed to a halt and struck a resounding blow on the wall to show how frustrated he was at missing his goal when he had got so near.

To this day, the monster's handprint can be seen on the wall of the castle at Sandell. MacDonald paid the sprightly tailor for his work, and gave him a handsome bonus for braving the haunted church. The laird liked his smart new trews, and never realised that some of the stitches were longer and less neat than the others.

Gold-Tree and Silver-Tree

There once lived a king who had a queen called Silver-Tree and a beautiful daughter called Gold-Tree. They all lived together happily until one day Silver-Tree and Gold-Tree were sitting by a pool and it took Silver-Tree's fancy to peer into the water and talk to the trout swimming there: "Silver trout in the pool, who is the most beautiful queen in the world?"

"Gold-Tree is the most beautiful," replied the fish.

Silver-Tree was mad with jealousy. She could not stand the fact that there was someone in the world—someone in her very family—who was more beautiful than she. She decided that she would get Gold-Tree killed, and to be sure the girl was dead, she would eat Gold-Tree's heart and liver. The queen was so mad with jealousy that she told her husband, begging him to kill their daughter and give her the heart and liver to eat.

At just this time it happened that a prince from a far country had come to ask for Gold-Tree's hand in marriage. The king, who was a good man, saw that the two young people loved each other, and saw his chance. He sent Gold-Tree away with the prince to be married. Then, when out hunting with his

men, he took a deer's heart and liver, and gave them to his wife. Once she had eaten these, Silver-Tree was cured of her jealousy.

All went well until the queen visited the pool and again asked the fish who was the most beautiful.

"Gold-Tree your daughter is the fairest," said the trout.

"But my daughter is long dead!" exclaimed the queen.

"Surely she is not. For she has married a fine prince in a far country."

When Silver-Tree asked her husband she found that what

the trout had said was true.

"Make ready the great ship, for I must visit my daughter," said Silver-Tree. And because she had seemed cured of her jealousy, the king let her go.

When Silver-Tree came to her destination, the prince was out hunting. Gold-Tree saw her mother arriving, and knew that her life was in danger. She called her servants, and they locked Gold-Tree in her room. But Silver-Tree was cunning. When she found her daughter locked in, she called sweetly, "Put your little finger through the keyhole, so your mother may kiss it."

As soon as Gold-Tree's finger appeared through the keyhole, the wicked queen took a dagger that she had dipped in poison and stuck it into Gold-Tree's finger. Straight away, the princess collapsed, and soon she was dead, the poisoned point still in her finger as she lay.

When Gold-Tree's husband came home, he was horrified at what had happened. He broke into the room and saw his young wife dead on the floor. So beautiful was the dead princess, that he had her body preserved, and locked in her room, and kept the key himself.

After some years had passed, the prince's grief faded a little, although he never smiled, and he decided to marry once again. He did not tell his second wife about Gold-Tree's body, but one day she found the key to the dead girl's room. She was curious to see the one part of her husband's castle that she had never entered, so, when no one was looking, she quietly opened the door and went in. When she saw the beautiful body laid out in the room, she realised at once that this must be Gold-Tree, the princess who had died so tragically, for she had heard the tale of the girl's death. As she approached the body she saw the poisoned dagger still sticking in the girl's finger. Yes, this must be Gold-Tree. Still curious, the second wife pulled at the dagger to remove it, and Gold-Tree rose, alive, just as she had been before her mother's visit.

The second wife went to the prince and said to him, "What would you give me if I could make you laugh again?"

"Truly, nothing could make me laugh, unless Gold-Tree was alive again," said the prince sadly.

"Then come to her room, and surely you will find her living."

They ran to the room together and the prince saw that it was true. The second wife was amazed at the change that came over her husband and knew that Gold-Tree was his true love.

"Now you have your true love back again," she said, "I must go away."

But the prince was so grateful to her that he would not let her go. He insisted that she remain in his household, alongside Gold-Tree.

Everything went well for them until Silver-Tree visited the pool once more. The queen was horrified when the fish told her that Gold-Tree was still the most beautiful woman in the world.

"But I stabbed Gold-Tree with poison and she is long dead," protested the queen.

"You stabbed her, but she is still alive," the fish replied.

And so Silver-Tree once more set sail to her daughter's home, and it happened that the prince was out hunting when she arrived. Gold-Tree saw her mother approaching, and quaked with fear at what she would do. "Let us go to meet her," said the second wife calmly, and they went together, as if to greet a welcome guest.

Silver-Tree held out a precious gold cup that she was carrying. "I bring a refreshing drink for my daughter," she said.

The second wife looked at her coldly. "In this country, it is the custom for the visitor to drink first," she said.

Silver-Tree raised the cup to her mouth, but hesitated, knowing that if she drank, she would kill herself. Just at that moment, the second wife's arm shot out and struck the cup, sending some of the deadly poison straight down Silver-Tree's throat. The wicked queen fell dead to the floor, and the servants took up her body to bury her. At last, Gold-Tree, the prince, and his second wife could live in peace.

The Frog

A widow was baking in her kitchen and asked her daughter to go down to the well to fetch some water. Off the daughter went, down to the well by the meadow, but when she came to the well she found that it was dry. She wondered what she and her mother would do without water, for it was high summer and there had not been a cloud in the sky for days. And the poor girl was so anxious that she sat down beside the well and began to cry.

Suddenly, through her sobbing, the girl heard a plop, and a frog jumped out of the well.

"What are you crying for?" asked the frog.

The girl explained that there was no water and she did not know what to do.

"Well," said the frog, "if you will be my wife, you shall have all the water you need."

The girl thought that the creature was making fun of her, so she went along with the joke, and agreed to be the frog's wife. She lowered her bucket into the well once more, and sure enough, when she pulled it up, the bucket was full of water.

The girl took the water back to her mother, and thought no more about the frog until it was evening. Then, as the girl and her mother were about to go to bed, they heard a small voice and a scratching sound at the door of their cottage: "Open the door, my own true love. Remember the promise you made to me, when fetching your water down at the well."

"Ugh, it's a filthy frog," said the girl.

"Open the door to the poor creature," said her mother, for she was a gentle woman who liked to be kind to animals. And so they opened the door.

"Give me my supper, my own true love. Remember the promise you made to me, when fetching your water down at the well," the frog went on.

"Ugh, I don't want to feed the filthy beast," said the daughter.

"Give the poor creature something to eat," insisted her mother. So they laid out some food and the frog ate it all up thankfully.

"Put me to bed, my own true love. Remember the promise you made to me, when fetching your water down at the well," said the frog.

"Ugh, we can't have that slimy thing in our bed," protested the daughter.

"Put the poor creature to bed and let it rest," said the mother. So they turned down the sheets and the frog climbed into bed.

Then the frog spoke again: "Bring me an ax, my own true love. Remember the promise you made to me, when fetching your water down at the well."

The widow and her daughter looked at each other in deep puzzlement. "What would the creature want with an ax?" asked the girl. "It is far too heavy for a frog to lift."

"Fetch him an ax," said the mother. "We shall see soon

enough." So the daughter went out to the woodshed and returned with the ax.

"Now chop off my head, my own true love. Remember the promise you made to me, when fetching your water down at the well," croaked the frog to the daughter.

Trembling, the girl turned to the frog, who stretched out his neck obligingly. She raised the ax high, just as she did when chopping wood for the fire, and brought it down on to the frog's neck. When she had done the deed, the girl looked away for a moment, scared to see the dead creature and its severed head. But when she heard her mother's shout of surprise she looked back quickly. And there stood the finest, most handsome young prince that either of them had ever seen.

"It was me you promised to marry," smiled the prince.

And the poor widow's daughter and the handsome prince *did* marry, and they lived in happiness for rest of their lives.

The Black Bull of Norway

Long ago in Norway there lived a woman, and she had three daughters. One day the eldest daughter went to her mother and said that she had decided to seek her fortune. So the girl went to see the old witch-washerwoman who could foretell people's futures. And the witch-washerwoman said to her, "Stand by my back door and see what you can see."

The first day, the girl could see nothing unusual outside the witch-washerwoman's back door, and nothing came on the second day. But on the third day, a fine coach pulled by six

horses appeared in the road beyond the back door. The girl went to the witch-washerwoman and told her what she had seen. "That's for you," said the witch-washerwoman, and the girl got into the coach and rode away.

Soon the second daughter decided she too should seek her fortune, and went to the witch-washerwoman's house, as her sister had done. The first day, she could see nothing unusual outside the witch-washerwoman's back door, and nothing came on the second day. But on the third day, a fine coach appeared. "That's for you," said the witch-washerwoman, and the second daughter rode away.

Then the youngest daughter followed in her sisters' footsteps, going to the witch-washerwoman's house in her turn. The first

day, she could see nothing outside the witch-washerwoman's back door, and nothing came on the second day. But on the third day, a great black bull appeared, bellowing as it walked. "That's for you," said the witch-washerwoman.

The girl was fearful of the great black creature, but in the end she plucked up the courage to climb on to the beast's back, and they galloped away together. The bull seemed kind, and when the girl felt hungry and asked for refreshment, the bull said, "Eat from out my right ear, and take drink from my left." The girl did so, and felt wonderfully refreshed.

By and by they came to a fine castle, and the bull slowed down at its gate. "Here lives my eldest brother," said the bull, and the two rested for the night at the castle. In the morning, the lord of the castle took the girl into a fine chamber, and gave her an apple. "Do not break into this apple until you are in the greatest need," said the lord. "Then it will help you."

The girl and the bull rode on for many miles more, until they arrived at a second castle, bigger and fairer than the first. "Here lives my second brother," said the bull, and the two rested there for the night.

In the morning, the lord of the castle took the girl into a fine chamber, and presented her with a pear. And he spoke to her rather as the first lord had done. "Do not break into this pear until you are in need," said the lord. "Then it will help you."

Once again the two traveled on, over hill and dale, until they came to a third castle, still finer and larger than the others. "Here lives my youngest brother," said the bull, and the lord of the castle once more gave them lodgings for the night.

In the morning, the lord of the castle took the girl into a fine chamber, and presented her with a plum. "Do not break into this fruit until you are in the greatest need," said the lord. "Then it will help you."

Off they went again, and after another long ride, the bull came to a halt in a dark and lonely glen. "This is where you

must get down," the bull said. "For the time has come when I must leave you to go and fight with the devil. Sit down on that stone and do not move from here, for if you move I shall not find you. Look around you, and if everything turns blue, I shall have won my fight with the devil; but if all turns red that will mean I have lost."

After a while everything in the glen turned blue, and the girl's heart was filled with joy that the bull had won his fight. So pleased she was that she moved one foot and crossed it over the other, quite forgetting the bull's instructions to stay absolutely still. So, no matter how long she sat, the bull could not find her again.

When the black bull did not return, the girl saw the reason, and she knew that she must complete her journey alone. So off she went along the glen, until she came to a great hill made all of glass. She walked around the hill, but could not climb it, for its glassy surface was so slippery. Finally she found a smith's house, and the smith told her that he would make her some metal shoes so that she could cross the hill in safety.

The girl climbed the glassy hill, and made her way carefully down the other side, and what should she see but the house of the old witch-washerwoman—her journey had brought her full circle. When she was talking to the washerwoman and her daughter, they told her of a handsome knight who had brought some bloodstained shirts to be washed. The blood had almost ruined the shirts, so he had promised to marry the woman who could wash away the stains, but neither the old washerwoman nor her daughter could do this, no matter how they rubbed and scrubbed.

The girl took the shirts and began to wash them, and both the washerwoman and her daughter turned green with envy as they saw the bloodstains disappearing. But when the knight returned for his shirts, the washerwoman told him that it was her daughter who had washed them. And so it happened that the knight and the washerwoman's daughter prepared to get married.

The girl wondered what to do, since she admired the

knight and desperately wanted the truth to be known. So she decided to break open the apple she had been given at the first castle. Out tumbled a heap of gold and jewels. "Delay your marriage for one day," said the girl to the washerwoman's daughter, "and you shall have these jewels."

The bride-to-be agreed, and the girl planned to go to the knight in the evening and explain the truth to him. But the washerwoman saw how things stood and gave the knight a sleeping-potion to drink. Through her tears, the girl sang a snatch of song:

The bloody shirt I washed for thee.
Will you not waken and turn to me?

Next day, the girl could think of nothing to do but break open her pear. Out came jewels even more precious than those that had come out of the apple. "Delay your marriage for one day," said the girl to the washerwoman's daughter, "and you shall have them all."

The washerwoman's daughter agreed, and the girl once more got ready to go to the knight. But once again the washerwoman gave

216

him a sleeping-potion, so that the truth could not be told him. Again the girl sang through her tears of sadness:

> The bloody shirt I washed for thee.
>
> Will you not waken and turn to me?

The knight heard nothing of this song. But the next day, when he was out hunting, one of his men said to him, "What was that singing and moaning last night outside your chamber?" The knight, curious to find out what was going on, was determined that nothing should make him fall asleep the next night.

Meanwhile, the girl broke open the plum, and still richer jewels fell out. These she offered to the washerwoman's girl, who again accepted them. But this time, the knight, who by now suspected the washerwoman, only pretended to drink.

So it was that the knight came to hear the truth. The girl who had ridden the black bull, climbed the hill of glass, and washed the blood-stained shirt finally married her knight. And the washerwoman's daughter was content with her jewels.

The Well at the World's End

There was once a king, a widower, and he had a daughter who was beautiful and good-natured. The king married a queen, who was a widow, and she had a daughter who was as ugly and ill-natured as the king's daughter was fair and good. The queen detested the king's daughter, for no one would notice her own girl while this paragon was beside her, so she made a plan. She sent the king's daughter to the well at the world's end, with a bottle to get some water, thinking she would never come back.

The girl walked far and was beginning to tire when she came upon a pony tethered by the roadside. The pony looked at the girl and spoke: "Ride me, ride me, fair princess."

"Yes, I will ride you," replied the girl, and the pony carried her over a moor covered with prickly gorse and brambles.

Far she rode, and finally she came to the well at the world's end. She took her bottle and lowered it into the well, but the well was too deep and she could not fill the bottle. Then three old men came up to her, saying, "Wash us, wash us, fair maid, and dry us with your linen apron."

So she washed the men and in return they lowered her bottle into the well and filled it with water.

When they had finished, the three men looked at the girl and spoke her future. "If she was fair before, she will be ten times more beautiful," said the first.

"A diamond and a ruby and a pearl shall drop from her mouth every time she speaks," predicted the second.

"Gold and silver shall come from her hair when she combs it," said the third.

The king's daughter returned to court, and to everyone's amazement, these predictions came true.

All were happy with the girl's good fortune, except for the

queen and her daughter. The queen decided that she would send her own daughter to the well at the world's end, to get her the same gifts. After traveling far, the girl came to the pony, as the king's daughter had done before her. By now, the beast was tethered once more. But when the creature asked her to ride it, the queen's daughter replied, "Don't you see I am a queen's daughter? I will not ride you, you filthy beast."

The proud girl walked on, and she soon came to the moor covered with gorse and brambles. It was hard going for the girl, and the thorns cut her feet badly. Soon she could hardly walk with the pain.

After a long and painful walk across the moor, the queen's daughter came to the well at the world's end. She lowered her bottle, but like the king's daughter, found that it would not reach the water in the well. Then she heard the three old men speaking: "Wash us, wash us, fair maid, and dry us with your linen apron."

And the proud daughter replied, "You

nasty, filthy creatures, do you think a queen's daughter can be bothered to wash you, and dry your dirty faces with my fine clean clothes?"

So the old men refused to dip the girl's bottle into the well. Instead, they turned to her and began to predict her future: "If she was ugly before, she will be ten times uglier," said the first.

"Each time she speaks, a frog and a toad will jump from her mouth," predicted the second.

"When she combs her hair, lice and fleas will appear," said the third.

With these curses ringing in her ears, the unhappy girl returned home. Her mother was distraught when she saw her daughter, for she was indeed uglier than before, and frogs, toads, fleas, and lice, jumped from her. In the end, she left the king's court, and married a poor cobbler. The king's fair and good-natured daughter married a handsome prince, and was happy—and good-natured—for the rest of her long life.

The Princess of the Blue Mountains

There was a poor widow who had one son called Will. Because he was all she had in the world she always let him have his way, and he became lazy. In the end she said to him, "Son, you must make your own way in the world. Then you will know what it is to find your own work and earn your own living." So young Will went off to seek his fortune.

Will traveled until he came to a fast-flowing river, which he had to cross. When he saw the rapid current and the sharp rocks, he was afraid to go into the water, and waited for a while. As he was standing there, a lady on the opposite bank saw him, and waved at him to cross, which finally he did.

When Will got to the other side, the lady said she would give him food and drink if he would go into her garden and find the most beautiful flower. But Will, struck by the lady's beauty, said "You are the fairest flower in all the garden."

The lady, already charmed by Will, turned to him. "Will you be my husband?" she asked. "There will be many dangers in store for you, but I'll try to help you through them."

222

Will looked at the lady and it did not take him long to say "Yes, I will be your husband, whatever dangers I must face."

Then the lady explained her story to Will. She was the Princess of the Kingdom of the Blue Mountains, and had been stolen away from her father's land by a demon called Grimaldin. For three nights, the demon would send his legions to do battle with Will. The lady gave Will three black sticks, one for each legion of demons, and a pot of ointment, in case he should be injured. "Use these things well, for now I must leave you."

As soon as the lady had left, three legions of demons appeared. They were armed with fearsome clubs, which they

raised to beat Will. But the young man stopped their blows, and used the lady's sticks to beat them off. Soon they were gone.

The next morning, the lady returned, and was pleased to see Will hale and hearty. "Well done. Never before has any man fought off the demons with such skill and courage. Tonight, twice as many demons will come to challenge you, so I will give you six sticks to help you fight them off." And the lady left once more, this time giving Will a larger pot of ointment, in case he should be wounded.

Sure enough, six legions of demons arrived to do battle with Will and again he beat them off successfully.

The lady greeted Will with gladness the following morning. "This time, I must give you twelve sticks, for twelve legions will come tonight. Look out of Grimaldin, for he will certainly come too." She left more ointment, for no one had survived a fight with Grimaldin without being sorely wounded.

Quickly Grimaldin and his whole army of twelve legions arrived, and the chief demon spoke to Will: "What is your business here?"

"I come to rescue the Princess of the Blue Mountains."

"Then you shall die."

Straightaway, the demons attacked, and Will beat them off

struck Will to the ground. The young man, sore and wounded all over, quickly applied the ointment. He was amazed to feel whole and well again, and stood up to face Grimaldin. This time, he beat off the chief demon, who went away, howling.

When the princess reappeared, she looked relieved. "Your greatest danger is over," she said to Will. "Take this book about the history of my family, and let no one distract you from reading it. If you know all that is in this book, you will be one of my father's favorites, and he will allow you to marry me."

Will started to read the book. He heard all sorts of voices trying to distract him, but he kept his eyes glued to the pages. Then he heard a woman coming by selling apples. Will liked nothing more than a ripe apple, so he looked up from the

nothing more than a ripe apple, so he looked up from the book. No sooner had he done so than he felt himself thrown against the apple woman's basket with such force that he passed out.

A while later, Will came to. The apple woman was gone and the princess was nowhere to be seen. There was an old man sitting nearby on a bench and Will asked him if he knew how to get to the kingdom of the Blue Mountains. The old man did not know, so he asked the fishes of the sea, and no fish knew the whereabouts of the kingdom. The old man said "I have a brother, five hundred years older than me, who can talk to the birds of the air. He will know, or will man's aged brother, and all the birds were called together. None knew where the kingdom of the Blue Mountains could be found, until the last bird, a great eagle, arrived. "I can take you to the kingdom," said the eagle. And Will climbed onto the great bird's back.

In the kingdom of the Blue Mountains, they landed near a house hung with black drapery. Will asked for lodgings, but the people at the house said that they could not help him. Their master was to be fed to a giant who terrorized the kingdom, asking for a human victim to eat every day. Anyone who could kill the giant would please the king, and would be given the hand of his daughter in marriage.

Will knew what he must do. He put on his armor, and strode out to challenge the giant. They fought long and hard, and Will was finally the winner. The princess recognized him and when the king learned that he had killed the giant, gave his permission for Will and the princess to marry. After the wedding, Will's mother came to live with them at the royal castle, and they were all happy together.

The Widow's Son and the King's Daughter

There was once a young lad called Jack, whose father died, leaving Jack and his mother without money. So, for the first time in his life, Jack had to go out to work. He had few useful skills, but he knew that he was no use to his mother at home, so set off one day to seek his fortune, whatever it might be.

After traveling a long way on the first day, Jack came across a house near a wood. He stopped and talked to the people of the house and, as he looked weak from his journey, they offered him food and a bed for the night. In the morning, the man of the house asked Jack if he needed work, and Jack replied that he did. "I have a herd of cattle that needs minding," said the man. "If you will do that job for me I should be pleased. But do not go into the field with the fruit trees. For a giant lives in that field and he will surely gobble you up if you go there. He may even carry off my cattle to eat."

Jack went to the field to mind the cattle, and he had not been there long when he started to admire the fruit on the trees in the neighboring field. There were red apples and ripe pears, as well as all sorts of other strange fruit that Jack did not recognise. He peered through the hedge and no one seemed to be about. So Jack thought he would risk a quick dash into the giant's field to take some fruit.

As Jack was picking some of the fruit, an old woman passed along the lane that ran by the edge of the field. She was also admiring the fruit, and asked Jack if he would pick some for her. Looking around him cautiously to make sure the giant was not coming, Jack agreed, and soon both he and the old woman had some fine, succulent fruit to eat.

"I will give you something useful in return for your favor," the old woman said to Jack. "Here are three stout rods and a

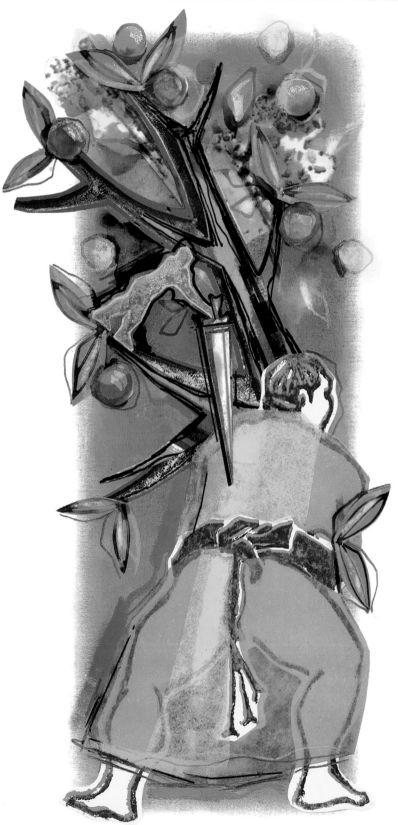

sword. Whoever you stab with this sword, they will be sure to fall down dead. You need never fear your enemies."

Jack thanked the old woman with all his heart, for in truth he had been worried about the giant, and wondered whether the beast would stride over the hedge into his field and take his revenge for the stolen fruit.

Sure enough, it was not long before the giant appeared. Jack hastily climbed a tree, for he had not tried the sword and wondered whether it would work. This did not put off the giant, who stepped towards the tree, held out his hand, and heaved. The tree was torn up by the roots, and Jack fell to the ground. But as the giant did this, Jack's sword grazed his flesh, and the giant fell down dead.

The next day, Jack was guarding his master's cattle again, when another giant appeared by the trees. "Do you dare to slay my brother?" the beast bellowed. Jack drew his sword and ran at the giant, felling the beast with one blow. As he looked at the massive corpse, Jack wondered if there were any more in the giant's family.

On the third day, another giant appeared. Jack hid himself in the hollow of a tree, and heard the creature grunting that he must have one of Jack's beasts to eat. "You will have to ask me first," shouted Jack from inside the hollow tree.

"Oh, is it you, who killed my two brothers?" roared the giant. "I shall take my revenge on you before long." But as the giant drew near the tree, Jack leaped out and stabbed him. The last of the giants was dead.

When he had got his breath back, Jack decided to go to the giants' castle, which was not far off, and see what riches might be hidden there. When he arrived, he told the giant's steward, who looked after the castle, that he had conquered the giants, and the steward, amazed at Jack's strength, gave the lad the keys to the castle treasuries. Jack took some of the money he found there and traveled back home to see his own people.

Jack found his country in turmoil when he arrived. People were weeping, and they told him that a fire-breathing monster had come to the country and had demanded one young boy or girl to eat every day. Tomorrow, it was the turn of the king's daughter, who would be killed by the beast if no one could slay the monster or drive it away.

Jack put on his armor and took his faithful sword. Then he went to see the princess whom the monster was hoping to devour. He told her that he had come to save her, and asked if she would marry him if he was successful. To this she agreed, and in relief, Jack fell at her feet and was soon asleep with his head in the princess's lap. While Jack was asleep, the princess wove a ringlet of white stones in his hair, as a good luck charm.

Suddenly, the monster crashed into the room. The princess started in fear and Jack woke up. In one movement he jumped up and drew his sword. Holding the weapon in front of him, he aimed many blows at the monster, but he could not get close enough to wound the beast because of the fire that came spurting from the creature's mouth. They carried on like this for some time, Jack waving his sword and the beast spitting fire, until the monster began to tire and slunk away.

The next day, the beast returned. The same thing happened,

with neither the beast nor Jack the winner, until the monster again grew tired and this time flapped its wings and flew away.

Jack thought hard. It was the creature's fire that caused the problem. So on the third day, Jack borrowed a camel, and made the animal drink several barrels of water. When the dragon appeared, Jack made the camel spit out its water to put out the fire. Then, before the monster could produce more flames, Jack went in for the kill, stabbing the beast and laying it low. At last the princess, and all her people, were saved.

Jack and the princess were betrothed, and Jack went away for some more adventures before his planned wedding day. After

nine months, the
princess had a baby, but
no one knew who the
father could be. The
king was angry with
his daughter, but she
persuaded him to go
with her to see a fairy,
who might be able to
give them the answer.
The fairy placed a
lemon in the child's
hand and said, "Only
the child's true father
will be able to take this
fruit from its hand."

The king then called
all the men in his
kingdom to the palace
and every one of them
tried to take away the
lemon. But no matter
how hard they tried,
the fruit would not

come away from the baby's hand. Finally, Jack appeared, and as soon as he touched the baby, the lemon came away.

The king was filled with anger towards Jack and his daughter, and wanted them to leave the palace forthwith. So he put the princess and Jack in rags and set them in a rotten boat and cast them out to sea. Just as the couple thought that they were going to sink, a lady appeared. "I was the fairy who gave Jack his sword, and the one who protected the princess from the breath of the beast," she said. "Once more, I will help you." She repaired the boat, turned their rags to fine robes, and so they returned to the palace.

Now Jack explained to the king who he was. "I was the man who saved your daughter from becoming the victim of the monster," said Jack. And Jack produced the king's gold cup, which he had taken before, and the monster's head, to show he spoke true. As further proof, the princess showed them all the ringlet of stones in Jack's hair. Convinced of the truth, the king allowed the couple to marry. They lived in happiness, and eventually, Jack himself became king.

Kate Crackernuts

Long ago there lived a king and a queen and each had a daughter. The king's daughter, Kate, was fairer than the queen's daughter, and the queen grew jealous of her. Soon the queen was plotting to find a way to spoil Kate's beauty.

The queen went to see a witch, who asked her to keep Kate from her food and to send the girl to her. So the next morning the queen sent Kate to the witch, to ask for some eggs. But Kate managed to snatch a bite to eat before she left the house. When Kate arrived, the witch said, "Lift the lid off that pot over there," and Kate obeyed. But nothing happened. "Tell your mother to keep the larder locked," said the witch.

So the queen knew that Kate had had something to eat, and was more careful on the next morning. Again Kate went to the witch, but on her way she saw some country people picking peas. They gave the hungry girl some peas to eat, so once more nothing happened when the witch asked Kate to open the pot.

On the third day the queen herself went with Kate to the witch, watching the girl all the way. When Kate lifted the lid of the pot, out popped the head of a sheep, and this instantly changed places with Kate's own head. The queen was satisfied at last.

When the queen's daughter saw Kate, she was sorry for her half-sister. So she put a cloth over Kate's head and announced: "Let us go and seek our fortunes, and see if anyone in the world can cure you." The two girls traveled far until they came to a great castle. Kate's sister did not feel well, so they hoped to find lodgings in the castle. When they asked some passersby, they found that it belonged to a king. They knocked on the door, and the guards let them in.

Once inside the castle courtyard, the girls told the people they were travelers far away from home and asked if they could have lodgings for

the night. They were soon granted their wish, as long as Kate would stay up at night to look after the king's sick son. A purse of silver was promised to Kate if she did this, and she readily agreed.

All went well until midnight. As the castle clock struck twelve, the prince began to climb out of bed. He put on his clothes, opened the door of his room, and went downstairs to the stables. Kate followed, but made sure that the prince did not see him, even when she jumped silently up on the horse behind him.

Off they rode through a forest, and as they went, Kate reached up into the trees and picked nuts from the branches, gathering them all in her apron. When they reached a green hill, the prince stopped his horse. "Open and let the prince enter," said the king's son. "And his lady too," said Kate, quietly.

One side of the green hill opened and they rode in. Kate saw

a fine hall, filled with lords and ladies who were dancing. Kate sat by the door, where she saw some fairies and a child playing with a wand. "Three strokes of the wand would make Kate's sister well," said one of the fairies. So Kate rolled nuts across the floor to the child until he forgot the wand, and Kate hid it in her apron.

Then a cock crew, the prince mounted his horse, and Kate jumped up behind. Together they rode back to the castle. As soon as she could, Kate tapped her sister three times with the fairy wand, bringing her back to health. Kate's sister then touched Kate with the wand. The sheep's head disappeared, and Kate's fair face returned. Then Kate sat by the fire, cracking her nuts, and eating them, as if nothing had happened. When the king asked her how she had fared with his son, she replied that he had had a good night. The king asked her to sit with him one night more, and he offered her a purse of gold

pieces in payment if she would.

So the next night saw Kate once more sitting by the prince's bedside, and, when the clock struck midnight, the prince went to his horse and rode again to the green hill, as before.

The king asked Kate to watch his son for one night more. "How shall I reward you this time?" asked the king.

"Let me marry your son if I look after him for a third night."

As on the two previous nights, the prince went to his horse at midnight and rode to the green hill. Kate sat quietly as the prince danced. Once·more, she noticed the small child who had had the wand. This time, he was playing with a bird, and Kate heard one of the fairies say, "Three bites of that bird would cure the prince." So Kate rolled nuts across the floor to the child until he forgot the bird, and Kate hid it in her apron.

They returned to the castle, and instead of cracking her nuts as before, Kate plucked the bird and roasted it. When he smelled the bird, the prince said "That smells very fine. I would like to have some of that meat to eat." Kate gave him one bite, and the prince rose up, supporting his weight on his elbow; she gave him a second bite, and he sat up in bed; she gave him a third bite and he got up, and sat by the fire.

When the king and the others came into the room they found the prince and Kate cracking nuts and eating them together. The prince looked as well as could be, and soon they were married. Meanwhile, the king's other son married the queen's daughter. They all lived in happiness, and were never again troubled by royal jealousy.

The Son of the King of Ireland

One day the son of the King of Ireland was out hunting, and brought down a raven. He looked at the bird's black feathers and red blood, and he said to himself, "I will not marry until I find a woman with hair as black as the raven's feathers, and cheeks as red as the raven's blood."

When he got home he told his father, who replied, "You will not easily find such a woman."

The youth said, "I will travel the world until I find her."

So the son of the King of Ireland set off on his search. Everywhere he went, he asked people if they had seen a woman with hair as black as the raven's feathers, and cheeks as red as the raven's blood. And he was told that the King of the Great World had three daughters, and that the youngest was just such a woman. So the lad determined to find her.

On his way, the lad called on a smith, who was making a great needle. "You are in luck," said the smith. "This needle I am making is for the King of the Great World himself. His boat comes tomorrow to collect it, and I will ask his men to ferry you across to his castle."

In the morning the boat came and the lad jumped on board. When they arrived at the castle, the lad, dusty with travel as he was, went straight to the King of the Great World, to ask him for one of his daughters in marriage.

"If you want to marry my daughter, you must be of nobler birth than you look," said the king.

"I am the son of the King of Ireland," the boy replied.

The King of the Great World paused. "You shall win the hand of my daughter," he said. "But you must do three things. First, clear all the filth from my great barn, and make it so clean that a gold ball will run from one end of the floor to the other."

The youth began to clear the barn. But no matter how much

filth he removed, more came in its place. Just then, the king's three daughters came by. They could see that the lad was harassed and could not finish his task.

The eldest daughter said, "If I thought it was me you wanted, I would clear the barn for you." And the middle one said the same.

But the youngest daughter said, "Whether you have come for me or not, I will clear the barn." She said, "Clean, clean, pitchfork, put out shovel." Straight away the whole floor of the barn was clean.

When the king returned, he said he was pleased with the boy's work and told him his next task. "Tomorrow you must thatch the barn with birds' feathers. I want the stem of every feather to point inwards and whole roof to be secured with a silk thread."

As soon as the lad got any feathers on the roof, a wind came and blew them away. Then, the king's three daughters came by. The eldest said, "If I thought it was me you wanted, I would thatch the barn for you." And the middle one said the same.

But the youngest daughter said, "Whether you have come for me or not, I will thatch the barn." She took out her whistle and blew. Straightaway, a beautiful, neat thatch of birds' feathers covered the roof of the barn, just as the king had ordered.

When the king saw the barn he said, "I am pleased with your

work. But I am not pleased with your teacher. You have more
work to do tomorrow. You must mind my five swans. If you let
any of them escape, you will be hanged, but if you keep them,
you shall have my daughter."

The boy tried to herd the swans together, but they always
escaped. Then, the king's three daughters came by. The eldest
said, "If I thought it was me you wanted, I would find the
swans for you." And the middle one said the same.

But the youngest daughter said, "Whether you have come for
me or not, I will find my father's swans." And she blew her
whistle, and the swans came home.

When the King of the Great World arrived, the lad said,
"Shall I get your daughter now?"

"Not yet," replied the king. "Tomorrow I am going fishing, and you must clean and cook the fish that I catch."

The next day the son of the King of Ireland began to scrape the scales from the fish. But no matter how many he removed, more appeared in their place. At that very moment, the king's three daughters came by. The eldest said, "If I thought it was me you wanted, I would clean the fish for you." And the middle one said the same.

But the youngest daughter said, "Whether you have come for me or not, son of the King of Ireland, I will clean the fish." And she cleaned the fish, saying, "My father will kill us both when he wakens. We must take flight together." And the pair

took flight, and galloped off together as fast as their steed could carry them.

Soon the king leapt on his horse, and gave chase. The lad and the princess heard the hooves of the king's horse beating on the ground behind them. The king's daughter said, "Look and see what you can find in the horse's ear."

"Just a little bit of thorn," said the lad.

"Throw it behind you," said the girl. At once, the thorn grew into a dense wood seven miles long. The king could not get through, until he called for an ax and hacked himself a path.

Again the daughter urged the lad, "Look in the horse's ear."

"A tiny stone," he said.

"Throw it behind you," she replied. And when he did, the stone turned into a massive rock, seven miles long and one mile high, and the couple were on the top.

The king could not climb the rock, so he returned home, and the couple went on their way to Ireland. As they approached the palace of the King of Ireland, the girl said, "I will not come in now. When you go in, the dog will jump up to welcome you. Try to keep him away, for if the dog touches your face, you will forget me."

So the couple went their separate ways. The daughter put on men's clothes and went to lodge with a smith who wanted a new apprentice. She stayed with him a year, and was soon the

best apprentice he had ever had.

Then a messenger arrived at the smithy, inviting the smith to the wedding of the son of the King of Ireland and the daughter of the King of Farafohuinn, and he decided to take his apprentice. "Please let me use the smithy tonight," said the daughter. By the following morning, she had made a hen of gold and a silver cockerel.

On the day of the wedding, the smith and his apprentice set off, she with the golden hen and silver cockerel, he with some grains of wheat in his pocket. Everyone was pleased to see them, and someone asked what they could do to entertain the guests. So the apprentice put the golden hen and the silver cockerel on the floor and threw down three grains of wheat. The cockerel picked up two grains, the hen only one.

"Do you remember how I cleaned the great barn for you? If you remembered, you would not take two grains instead of one," said the hen.

Everyone laughed, and they threw down another three grains. The same thing happened. "Do you remember when I thatched the barn with birds' feathers?" asked the hen.

As they threw down more grains, the son of the King of Ireland began to remember what had happened to him.

"Do you remember how I found the swans for you? If you remembered, you would not take two grains instead of one."

Now the king's son was sure. "It must be you," he shouted, and they undid the apprentice's costume to show that she was indeed a woman.

The son of the King of Ireland turned to the princess of Farafohuinn, who he was going to marry, and said "This is truly the woman I went in search of. I passed through many tests and trials for her, and I will marry none but her. Stay and celebrate with us if you wish, but otherwise you may go."

So the princess of Farafohuinn left the castle, and the Son of the King of Ireland at last married his true love.

The Black Horse

There was a king who had three sons, and when he died the youngest son was left nothing except a horse, an old, white mare with a limp. The young son realized that he would get nothing more, so he decided to leave home.

Off he went, sometimes riding the mare, sometimes walking to rest her, when he met a man riding a black horse. The two greeted each other, and the man with the black horse spoke: "I have had enough of this black beast. Will you swap him for your horse? There is one great advantage to this black horse. Wherever in the world you wish to go, he will take you there."

The king's son thought of all the places that he wished to go, and could not resist the bargain. So he exchanged his old limping horse for the stranger's mount, and went on his way.

Now the king's son had long wanted to visit the Realm Underwaves, so he decided to see if the black horse would take him. Sure enough, before the sun had risen the next day, they were there. The King Underwaves was holding court, and trying to find someone who would go to Greece, for the Prince Underwaves wanted to marry the king's daughter.

The rider of the black horse stepped forward. "Will you go to Greece to fetch the king's daughter?" asked the King Underwaves. And before he knew what he was doing, the young rider of the black horse was on his way.

As he rode, the black horse spoke to him. He explained that no one in Greece had seen a horse before, and the princess would surely want a ride. "But beware. Tell her that no man except you may ride, for some rascal may try to steal me."

When they arrived in Greece, it was just as the black horse had said. The princess saw the horse out of one of the castle windows and straightaway asked for a ride. When she tried to ride the steed with her own servant, the black horse threw the man from his back. So the princess of Greece set off to the Realm Underwaves, and the only man to go with her was the horse's rightful rider.

Soon they arrived in the Realm Underwaves, where the prince was eager to arrange his wedding. But the Greek princess spoke up. "The wedding must not be so soon," she said. "I will not marry until I have the silver cup that my mother used at her wedding, and her mother before her."

The Prince Underwaves turned to the rider of the black horse. "Go back to Greece, and bring the silver cup to me before dawn tomorrow." So the black horse and his rider set off once more. As they traveled, the horse told his rider what he should do. "All the king's people will be around him tonight, and the silver cup will be passed among them. Go in with them, pretend to be one of the people of the place, and take the cup when it is handed to you. Then we will be away."

It all happened as the horse had said, and they were soon back in the Realm Underwaves with the silver cup. But when the prince began to talk of his wedding, the Greek princess spoke up once more. "I will not marry until I have the silver ring that my mother wore at her wedding, and her mother before her."

The Prince Underwaves turned to the rider of the black horse. "Go back to Greece, and bring the silver ring to me

before dawn tomorrow." So the black horse and his rider set off. As they traveled, the black horse told his rider what to expect on the journey. "This is a difficult quest," said the horse. "Before we can get the ring, we will have to climb a mountain of snow, a mountain of ice, and a mountain of fire."

On they rode, and the young man was amazed at the great leaps the horse took to climb the mountains of snow and ice. Perished with cold, he clung on to the creature's mane as he made his third leap. This took them through the mountain of fire, and so fast they went that they hardly felt the heat from the flames. "Now," said the horse. "Go into that town and make an iron spike for the end of every bone in my body, and

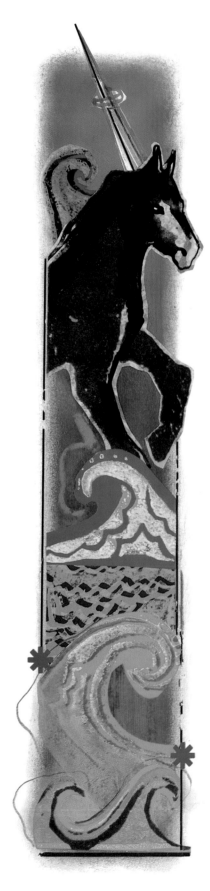

then stick the spikes into me as I tell you." The young man was puzzled, but he went to the smith and got the spikes made, and stuck them into the horse's body as he had been told.

"Near here there is a great loch," said the horse. "Watch the waters when I dive in, and you will see them covered in flames. If you see the flames go out, wait for me, and I will come to you with the ring."

The young man stood by as the horse disappeared beneath the water. Suddenly, the waters turned into bright orange flames. The young man waited and waited, but the flames still burned. He began to doubt whether he would see the black horse again. Then, just before dawn, the flames on the lake went out and the black horse appeared. There was one metal spike left, on the creature's head, and on this spike was the silver ring.

Without delay, they returned to the Realm Underwaves. Again the prince started to ask when the wedding might be, but the princess of Greece had yet one more demand. "I will not marry until you build a castle for me," she said.

The Prince Underwaves looked upset. A castle would take years to build. But the black horse said, "This is the easiest of all the tasks. Leave it to me." And before long an army of diggers, stone masons, carpenters, and metalworkers, were at work before them, until a fine castle was built before dawn the following day.

The rider of the black horse, the Prince Underwaves and the princess of Greece stood looking at the castle, which had its own deep well. "It is a fine castle," said the princess. "But there is still one problem with my wedding arrangements."

"What is that?" asked the prince.

"You," said the Greek princess, and pushed the prince into the well. "If I must be married, then, I want to marry the rider of the black horse, who has done deeds of craft and valor for me while the other man stood by."

And so it was that the young rider of the black horse married the princess of Greece, and lived in the new castle which the black horse had made for them.

Three years passed and the young rider, in his happiness, neglected the black horse. One day, as he saw the horse grazing where he had left him, the young man felt sorry for forgetting the beast that had given him so much help. "It seems as if you have someone that you prefer to me," said the horse.

"I am sorry that I forgot you," said the young man.

"It does not matter," said the horse. "Draw your sword and chop off my head, and that will be an end to it."

The young man protested,

but the horse would not take no for an answer, so the young man drew his sword and cut off the horse's head with one stroke. Straight away, the horse vanished, to be replaced by a handsome young man. "Good day to my brother-in-law," he said, and the rider of the black horse stared in puzzlement.

"You look sad to lose the horse," said the stranger. "But I hope you will be pleased to meet your brother-in-law. I was the black horse, and have been put under a spell. I used my knowledge of my father's house to help you. What is more, you kept me long and well, and, since I was put under the spell, I never met any other man who could keep me. Thank you for releasing me from the spell and giving me back my true shape." And the rider of the black horse was thankful. For now he had both a fine wife and a true friend.

The Greek Princess and the Young Gardener

There was once an old king who had one daughter. When the king grew ill it seemed as if the end of his life was coming, but he discovered that the apples from the tree in his garden made him better. So the king became angry when a strange, brightly colored bird flew into his garden one evening and began to steal the apples.

The king called his gardener. "You are not doing your job properly!" exclaimed the king. "You must guard my apple tree day and night, for a bird is coming into the garden and stealing all the fruit."

"It will not happen again, your majesty," replied the gardener. "I will set my three sons to guard the tree. And if the bird comes near, they will shoot it with their bows and arrows."

That night, the gardener's eldest son stood guard by the apple tree. As the night went on, the boy got drowsy, and soon he was asleep at the foot of the tree. At midnight, the bird flew into the garden and removed one of the fruit. The king heard the flapping of the bird's wings, for he was a light sleeper, and dashed to his window. When he looked out, the king saw the bird taking off with one of the finest fruits in his beak. "Wake up, you lazy good-for-nothing!" he shouted at the gardener's son. The lad grabbed his bow and arrow, but by the time he had taken aim it was too late. The bird had got away.

The next night, the gardener's second son was on guard. Again the lad fell asleep and again the bird came to steal an apple. The king roared at the gardener's boy, but by the time the lad had woken, the bird had flown away again, and another of the king's finest, most succulent apples was gone from the tree. The king began to despair.

On the third evening, the gardener's youngest son stood guard. He was determined to keep awake and do himself credit with the king. As usual the bird arrived and the boy was quick enough to let loose one arrow at the bird as it flew. He did not bring the bird down, but as his arrow fell to the ground, one of the creature's feathers fell with it.

The king was pleased, for the bird had not had the chance to steal an apple before it was frightened away by the young lad's arrow. But when he saw the feather, the king was fascinated. It was made of the finest beaten gold. As he looked at it, the king decided that he wanted to catch the bird with the golden feathers. So he sent out a message. He would give half his kingdom, plus the hand of his daughter in marriage, to any man who could bring back the bird to his palace.

All the young men of the king's household, including the gardener's three sons, wondered how they could find the bird. The gardener's first son was out one day when he met a fox. "If you want to find the golden bird," said the fox, "go along this road and take lodging with the poor man and his wife." So the boy went along the road, but when he came to the poor man's house, there was a house opposite where people were drinking and dancing, and the gardener's first son went there for his entertainment.

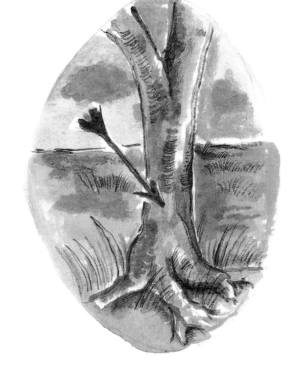

The same thing happened to the gardener's second son, who also met the fox and was given the same advice. But the drinking and dancing was of more interest to him, and he joined his brother.

When the third son met the fox, the animal gave him the same advice. Unlike his brothers, the young lad listened to what the fox had to say, and sought lodgings with the poor couple, and the next morning went on his way. Soon he met the fox once more. "Well done for taking my advice," said the fox. "Do you know where to find the golden bird?"

"I have no idea," said the young man.

"She is in the palace of the King of Spain, some two hundred miles from here," said the fox.

The gardener's son was sad to hear that the journey was to be so long.

"Do not despair," said the fox. "Hop up on my tail, and we shall soon be there."

So off they went, and to the young gardener's surprise, they soon got to the King of Spain's palace. The fox turned to the lad again and told him where in the palace to find the golden bird. "Get the bird out as quickly as you can, and do not stay looking for other treasure," said the fox. "Then you will be safe."

The youth entered the palace and found the bird in a dull iron cage. Next to it was a fine golden cage, and the lad thought that this would be a better home for the marvelous bird. So he tried to tempt the creature into the golden cage. But all that happened was that the bird let out a terrible squeal, and the palace guards came running. Soon, the boy found himself in front of the King of Spain himself.

"I should hang you for a thief," said the king. "But I will give you a chance to win your life, and the golden bird too if you succeed. Get me the bay filly belonging to the King of Morocco, a horse that can run faster than any other. Then you shall have the golden bird."

So the young gardener found his friend the fox, and they were soon on their way to the palace of the King of Morocco.

When they arrived the fox spoke to the lad again, more sternly than before. "When you get into the stables, do not touch a thing, not even the door or the door posts. Just lead out the bay filly, and you will be fine."

But when he entered the stable, the boy saw a fine golden saddle, much better than the leather one on the filly's back, so he decided to change it over. No sooner had he touched the golden saddle than palace guards appeared from every quarter. In a few moments, the King of Morocco himself had arrived.

"I should hang you for a thief," said the king. "But there is one thing that I want, and if you can help me, then I will let you go, and the bay filly with you." And the king explained that he wanted to marry Golden Locks, the daughter of the King of Greece, and asked the gardener's boy to go to Greece and bring back the princess.

Once again, the lad and the fox set off, and again the speed of the fox was such that by nightfall they arrived at the king's palace. "Do not let her touch anything or anyone as you come out," warned the fox.

The lad found the princess and quietly explained that he wanted to take her to Morocco. At first, she was unwilling to go on such a long journey to a husband she had never met, but as she looked at the young gardener, her heart began to melt and she agreed to go with him. "Only let me kiss my father goodbye," she said. The princess went to kiss her sleeping father, promising not to waken him. But as soon as her lips touched her father's he let out a great cry, and guards came running.

When he saw that his daughter was safe, he listened to the young gardener's story. He was sad to let his daughter go, for he had already lost his son, who had been spirited away by a wicked witch. "I will only let her go if you will clear up the great heap of clay in front of my palace," said the king. For no one had been able to clear the heap before, which got larger with every shovelful of clay that was removed.

To everyone's great astonishment, including that of the young

gardener, the pile of clay was cleared. The lad knew that the fox must have had something to do with it. So the young gardener, the princess and the fox went on their way.

By the time they reached the King of Morocco's palace, the young gardener and the princess were in love. When the king brought out his bay filly to exchange for the princess, the pair looked at each other with longing. "Please let me say farewell to the princess before I depart," said the lad. While the king was distracted, the pair jumped up on the horse and rode off at top speed, the bay filly galloping faster than the wind. When they reached the King of Spain's palace, the fox was there waiting for them.

The fox turned to them before they entered the palace.

"If you give the king the filly, I will have to carry you all home, and I doubt that I have the strength. When you are about to hand over the horse, go up to the creature and stroke it, as if you are saying farewell. Then, when the king is distracted, jump on the filly's back and ride away at top speed. Then we shall return in comfort."

The king brought out the golden bird, and handed it to the gardener's boy. Instead of giving the king the filly, as he expected, the boy rode out of the palace gates, leaving the king behind him in amazement. Soon he had met up with the fox and the princess once more, and the three returned to the homeland of the young gardener.

They finally reached the spot where the lad had first met the fox, and he turned to the creature to thank him for all his help. "Now will you help me?" asked the fox. "Take your sword and chop off my head and tail." The young man could not do this to his friend, but his eldest brother, who had come to meet them, knew nothing of how the fox had helped his brother, and dealt the two blows.

The head and tail vanished, and in place of the fox was a young man. Straight away, the Greek princess recognized her brother, who had been taken away and bewitched.

If they were happy before, the Greek princess and the young gardener were now overjoyed, and they longed to share their joy with the king. So the three of them went to see the old king and his daughter, gave the king his golden bird, and told them the whole story. The Greek princess married the young gardener, and the Greek prince married the daughter of the old king. The king himself was enchanted with his golden bird. He was so pleased with the creature, he even shared with it some of the apples from his favorite tree.

Canobie Dick

Canobie Dick was a horse trader who was well known for always getting the best deal. He did not care who he did business with, so long as he got more than he paid for every piece of horseflesh that passed through his hands.

It happened one night that Dick was riding home across Bowden Moor by the Eildon Hills. He had with him two horses that he had not been able to sell that day. As he rode he saw a figure in the distance, coming towards him. As the man got nearer, Dick saw that he was an old fellow, wearing clothes that looked positively ancient. Dick was surprised when the old man wished him good day and asked if the horses were for sale. Soon they struck a deal, and the old man paid Dick a good price in ancient gold coins. Normally Dick would have refused old coins, but he knew that gold was valuable in whatever form it came, so he took the payment readily.

A few times more Dick met the man and sold him horses, the old man always asking that Dick come at night to make the sale. When this had happened several times, Dick decided that he should get to know this customer better, and he said to the man, "A bargain is always luckier when struck with a glass in hand."

So it was that the old man invited Dick to his home, but warned him, "Don't be afraid at what you see in my dwelling-place, for if you do you'll be sorry for the rest of your life."

Off they went along a narrow path up the hills until they came to a rocky outcrop. To Dick's surprise, the old man passed through a passage into the hillside. Although Dick had often passed this place, he had never noticed the passage before.

"You are sure you are not afraid?" said the old man.

"It is not too late to turn back."

Dick shook his head, for he did not wish to seem frightened. The passage was lit by flaming torches, and as they walked along, Dick saw a long row of stables, with a black horse in each. Next to each horse lay a knight in black armor. Nearby was an old table, and on it were a horn and a sword.

"The man that blows this horn and draws this sword shall become king of the whole of Britain," said the man.

Dick looked at the sword in fascination, lifted it briefly, but put it down again. For when he thought of the sleeping figures and the ghostly horses, he thought that drawing the sword might bring all the terrors of the mountain down upon him.

So he raised the horn to his lips and got ready to blow.

But Dick was shaking so much, and he was so breathless with fear, that all he could produce was a feeble, wavering note. Even so, this was enough to rouse the knights who were resting next to their horses. Great rumbles of thunder echoed through the rocky hall, the horses seemed to come to life and the knights rose up, their armor clanking and their swords glittering in the torch light. Once they saw the knights rise up, the horses began to neigh and stamp their hooves, tossing their heads in excitement.

The horse dealer looked at the growing army of knights and horses, coming to life around him, looking as if they were all about to launch an attack on him. Trembling, he dropped the horn, and made a grab for the great sword on the table. As he did so, a mighty voice spoke from among the knights:

> The coward shall rue the day he was born
> Who lay down the sword and blew on the horn.

As he heard these words, Dick was picked up by a mighty whirlwind that blew along the cavern and cast him out onto the open hillside. There he lay unconscious until a group of shepherds found him in the morning.

Dick told the shepherds his tale, but died soon afterwards. And no one found the passage into the hillside again.

The Knight of Riddles

Once there was a king called Ardan, king of all Albann, and his first wife died. Some time afterwards, he remarried, and the king had two sons, one from each queen. The two boys were very close, but the second queen was jealous of the king's first son, because she knew that her own boy would not inherit the kingdom. So she plotted to kill the elder son.

Twice the queen ordered her servant to put poison in the elder son's drink, and twice her own son overheard her giving the orders, and warned his brother. Then the elder son said to his brother, "I shall not live long if I stay in this house. It will be better for me if I leave home." And so the two brothers decided that they would leave together.

When they left, they took their mother's poisonous drink with them in a bottle, and before long, the eldest said, "It might not be poison after all. Let us try it on my horse." When they gave the poison to the beast, it keeled over and died.

"Well, she was a tired old nag anyway," said the elder brother. "Her time was up. Let's try the drink on your steed." So they gave the poison to the other horse, which fell down dead.

The brothers decided that at least they would skin the horse to make a blanket to keep themselves warm. While they were preparing the skin, twelve ravens flew down to feast on the carcass. But no sooner had they begun to eat than the birds fell dead from the poisoned meat.

The brothers took the dead birds with them, and when they reached the next town, they asked the baker to make twelve pies from the ravens' flesh. They packed up the pies and carried on with their journey. At night the brothers came to a dense, dark wood, and they were set upon by twenty-four robbers. "Give us your money!" demanded the thieves.

"We have no money," said the brothers. "All we have are

these meat pies."

"Food is as good as money. We will take the pies."

Greedily, the robbers began to eat the pies, and before long, they were falling down dead where they stood, for the poison was still in the meat. Relieved, the brothers went on with their journey, until they came to a fine house, which was the home of the Knight of Riddles. They decided to visit the knight, and the younger brother said that he would pretend to be the servant to the elder.

The Knight of Riddles had a beautiful daughter attended by twelve maidens. He would allow no one to marry the girl unless they could give him a riddle which he could not solve. When they heard this the brothers decided to put this riddle to him: "One killed two, and two killed twelve, and twelve killed twenty-four, and two got out of it."

The brothers stayed in the knight's house while he tried to think of an answer to the riddle, and meanwhile each of the maidens came to the younger brother and asked him what the answer to the riddle might be. They brought him gifts of cloth, but he would not tell them. "Only my brother may tell the answer," he said.

Then the knight's daughter went to the elder brother, and smiled winningly at him, and presented a gift of cloth to him, and he told her the answer to the riddle. Not long afterwards, the knight called the brothers to him and told them that he had solved the riddle.

"Your riddle was easy to solve," said the knight. "Your head will be chopped off in the morning."

"Before you behead me," said the elder brother, "I have another riddle for you. My servant and I were in the forest shooting. He shot twelve hares, skinned them, and let them go. Then came a hare finer than the rest. I shot her, skinned her, and let her go."

"That's not a difficult riddle," said the knight. And they all knew that the young man had discovered how the knight found the answers to his riddles.

The brothers had defeated the knight in their battle of the riddles, so the knight allowed the elder brother to marry his daughter. The elder prince was so full of joy that he told his brother to go home and inherit his kingdom; he would stay in the land of the Knight of the Riddles.

The elder brother did well in the country of the knight and lived there for many years. The local people were impressed at his bravery, especially when he killed three giants that were causing fear in the land. So the Knight of the Riddles gave his son-in-law his own title, the Hero of the White Shield.

The Hero of the White Shield became famed as the strongest and bravest man in the land. Many challenged him to a fight, but no one could beat the Hero. One day, a stranger came to challenge him and, after a long fight, the stranger sent the Hero jumping in alarm over a high stone wall.

"You must have some of my own fighting blood in your veins to be so strong," said the Hero of the White Shield.

"What is your family?"

"I am the son of Ardan, king of all Albann," replied the stranger. And the Hero of the White Shield knew that he had met his long-lost brother once more. The two stayed for years together in the land of the Knight of Riddles. But eventually the younger brother knew that he should return to his own kingdom, so the two parted.

On the way home, the younger brother stopped to watch twelve men playing at shinny by a tall palace. For a while he joined in, but soon the smallest of the twelve grappled with him and shook him as if he were no more than a child. "Whose sons are you, who are so strong?" he asked.

"We are the nephews of the Hero of the White Shield," they cried. And the younger brother knew that he had found his sons, and that all were alive and well. They went together to find his wife, and a great celebration was held. For hundreds of years, the kings of Albann were descended from their line.

The Humble-Bee

Two young men were out walking one summer's day and stopped by a tiny stream next to an old ruined house. They were admiring the place, and noticed how the stream turned into a miniature waterfall crossed by narrow blades of grass. One of the men was tired from the walk and the afternoon heat and sat down by the stream. Soon he was fast asleep, and the other sat quietly, watching the view.

Suddenly, a tiny creature, about the size of a humble-bee, flew out of the sleeper's mouth. It landed by the stream and crossed it by walking over some grass stalks which hung over the water at its narrowest point. The creature then approached the ruin and disappeared into one of the cracks in the wall.

The man who saw all this was shocked and decided to wake his friend to see if he was all right. As he shook his companion awake, he was astonished to see the tiny creature emerge from the ruin, fly across the stream and re-enter the sleeper's mouth, just as the young man was waking.

"What's the matter? Are you ill?" asked the watcher.

"I am well," replied the sleeper. "You have just interrupted the most wonderful dream, and I wish you had not woken me

with your shaking. I dreamed that I walked through a vast grassy plain and came to a wide river. I wanted to cross the river to see what was on the other side, and I found a place near a great waterfall where there was a bridge made of silver. I walked over the bridge and on the far bank was a beautiful palace built of stone. When I looked in, the chambers of the palace contained great mounds of gold and jewels. I was looking at all these fine things, wondering at the wealth of the person who left them there, and deciding which I would bring away with me. Then suddenly you woke me, and I could bring away none of the riches."

The Seal Woman

The was a farmer from Wastness who was not married. His friends used to tease him when he said he was not interested in women, but he took little notice. His only interest was his farm, which did well, and the good farmer grew rich.

One day the farmer was walking by the shore at the ebb tide, and he noticed a group of seal folk. Some were sunning themselves on a rock, others were swimming and playing in the sea. The seals were enjoying themselves and did not notice the farmer, so he crept closer and saw that they had all taken off their sealskins to reveal bodies which were as pale and white as his own.

The farmer thought what fun it would be to catch one of the **naked seals, so he edged closer and then made a dash for the**

seals. They grabbed their skins in alarm and jumped into the water, but the farmer managed to hold on to one of the skins.

He watched as the seals swam out to sea and then turned to walk homeward across the shore. As he went he heard a sound of sobbing behind him, and turned to see a sealwoman, weeping for her lost skin. "Oh, please give me back my skin," she cried. "I cannot join my family in the sea without it."

The farmer was filled with pity, but he was also smitten by the beauty of the seal woman, whom he thought far more attractive than any ordinary woman. So he talked to the seal woman, and told her his feelings, and soon he persuaded her to come ashore and live with him as his wife.

The sealwoman lived long with the farmer. She was as a good a farmer's wife as any normal woman, and bore him seven children, four boys and three girls. She seemed happy and people often heard her singing, but she would sometimes look with longing at the sea.

One day the farmer took his three eldest sons out in his boat to go fishing, as they often did. While they were at sea, the seal-woman sent out three of her other children to walk the shore gathering limpets and whelks. The youngest daughter stayed at home, with her mother, because the girl's foot was sore and she could not walk far.

Once they had all gone out the sealwoman started to search the house. At first she made as if she was tidying up, but her daughter realised that she was looking for something, and said to her mother, "What is it that you are looking for all around the house?"

"You must tell no one my dear," said the sealwoman. "I am looking for a fine skin to make a dressing for your sore foot."

And the young girl replied, "I think I might know where you can find such a skin. One day when you were out and father thought we were asleep in bed, I saw him take a skin and look at it. Then he folded it carefully and hid it away up in the eaves above the bed."

Straightaway the seal woman rushed to the place and took out the skin from under the eaves. "Farewell my little one," she said as she rushed out of the door and ran in the direction of the shore. There she put on her skin, dived into the sea, and swam quickly away. A male seal saw her coming and greeted her with excitement, for he recognized the seal he had loved

long ago.

As the farmer was returning to shore in his boat, he saw his wife diving into the sea and making for the male seal. "Farewell, dear husband," she called to him. "I liked you well and you treated me kindly. But it is time that I returned to my true love of the sea."

That was the last the farmer saw of the seal woman. He missed his seal-wife greatly, and it took him many years to recover from his sadness. And he often went for walks along the shore, hoping to catch sight of her again.

Rashen Coatie

There was a king whose queen died young, and after a time he remarried. His new queen was a widow, and both king and queen had a daughter from their first marriage. The king's daughter, Rashen Coatie, was good and beautiful, while the daughter of the queen was ill-featured and bad-tempered.

The queen treated the king's daughter badly in the hope that her own girl would gain. Her husband, anxious to keep the peace at home, turned a blind eye to this ill-treatment, and so it came about that Rashen Coatie ended up looking after the king's cattle, while the queen's daughter stayed at home and wallowed in luxury.

Every day the queen sent her own daughter with the worst food for Rashen Coatie to eat, in the hope that the girl would fall ill and die. But Rashen Coatie met a fairy, who taught her a spell. Whenever the girl said the magic words, a calf appeared, bringing her food as fine as any that was eaten in the king's palace. In this way, Rashen Coatie became stronger and more beautiful than ever, and the queen became angrier and angrier.

When it was clear that her plan was failing, the queen went to talk to a witch. The witch gave the queen the power to look into the unknown, and the envious woman quickly realised that it was the calf who was giving Rashen Coatie her food.

Straight away she went to her husband and asked him to have the calf killed, so that she might cook the animal for a banquet, and the king agreed. Rashen Coatie was distressed when she heard what was to happen, but the calf came to her and spoke in her ear. "If you do what I say you need not worry," said the calf. "When I am cooked and eaten, take my bones and bury them under this stone. Do this, and leave the palace

for a while, and you will be safe."

Rashen Coatie buried the bones beneath the stone, left the palace, and went into hiding. The calf came back to life and brought her food and so she was able to survive. Meanwhile, the queen was poisoned when she ate the calf's entrails and, after a long illness, finally died.

By this time, Rashen Coatie was grown into a fine young woman. She did not know how well she would be received at her father's court, so decided to return in disguise. But when she arrived she was thrown into confusion. Her father was so taken with her beauty that he wanted to marry her. She ran to the calf to ask him what to do.

"Ask the king for clothes made of the rushes that grow by the stream," said the calf. The king had just such a dress made, and still he wanted to marry Rashen Coatie.

"Ask the king for a dress of all the colors of the birds of the air," said the calf. The king gave her a dress with all the colors **of the birds of the air, and still he wanted to marry her.**

"Ask the king for a dress, with the colors of all the fish of the sea," said the calf. But again the king produced just such a dress, and still he wanted to marry Rashen Coatie.

So finally the girl felt she had used up all the possible excuses to delay, and the wedding day arrived. When she got to church, Rashen Coatie tried one last objection. "I must have

the ring my mother wore when she was married," she said. And then she put on her dress of rushes, and ran from her father's kingdom.

After long wandering, Rashen Coatie came to a hunting lodge which belonged to a prince. No one seemed to be there, so exhausted, she collapsed on to the prince's bed, and fell into a deep sleep. Later, the prince himself arrived and found Rashen Coatie asleep on his bed. He woke the girl and asked what she was doing there. "I meant no harm," she said. "I am far from home and was tired and lost. Is there some place near here where I might find work?" So the prince took Rashen Coatie home and she was put to work in the palace kitchens.

Soon it was Christmas and all the people in the palace, from the prince to his lowliest servants, went to church in the morning. Only Rashen Coatie was left in the kitchen to turn the roasting spits.

She too wanted to go to church, and decided to use a spell the calf had taught her so the spits would turn themselves:

Every spit turn on your way

Until I return on this yule day.

And with that, Rashen Coatie put on her finest dress and ran off to church.

In church, the prince was entranced by the beautiful young

woman who entered just as the service was beginning. Little did he guess that it was the kitchen maid Rashen Coatie. The prince decided to speak to her as she left the church, but she slipped out quickly and ran back to the palace, hoping that none would know that she had left the kitchen.

But as the girl flew along the path, one of her tiny golden shoes came off and she left it behind in her haste. The prince knew now what he should do. "The woman whose foot fits this shoe shall be my bride," he said.

Hundreds of women came to the palace, but no foot fitted the shoe perfectly. Then the witch's daughter appeared, and she had pared her nails and even rubbed some of the skin off her heels, so that she could squeeze on the shoe. The prince knew that she was not the woman he had seen, but he was true to his word, and announced that he would marry the girl. But a small bird fluttered over the prince's head, singing:

> Clipped the heel and pared the toe;
> In the kitchen the shoe will go.

The prince turned back and ran to the kitchen, finding Rashen Coatie, who had not tried on the shoe. When it fitted, the prince went to church with his rightful bride.

The Tale of Ivan

Ivan was a poor man who had no work. So one day he left his wife to look for a job. After a while he came to a farm and the farmer agreed to take Ivan on and give him lodgings.

Ivan worked on the farm for a year, and the master said, "Ivan, you have worked well this year. It is now time for you to be paid. Will you be paid in money or advice?"

"I would prefer to take my wages in money," said Ivan.

"I would prefer to give you advice," said the master. "Never leave the old road for the new one." So Ivan had to be content with this piece of advice, and worked for his master another year.

At the end of the second year, the same thing happened. This time, the master told Ivan, "Never lodge where an old man is married to a young woman." Again Ivan had to be content with the advice.

After a third year, the master gave Ivan a third piece of advice, "Honesty is the best policy." By now, Ivan saw that he would get no money from this master, so he decided to take his leave and return to his wife. Maybe there would be work

nearer home.

"Very well," said the master. "I will give you a cake to eat on your journey."

Ivan set off and soon he fell in with a group of merchants who were returning home from a fair. He got on well with the merchants, but when they came to a fork in the road, the men wanted to travel along the shorter, straighter, new road. Ivan remembered his master's first piece of advice. "I prefer the old road," said Ivan, and they parted company.

Before long, the merchants were set upon by robbers. Ivan

could see what was happening, for the new road was visible from the old. "Robbers! Stop thief!" he bellowed at the top of his voice. When the robbers heard this, they ran off, and the merchants kept hold of their money.

After many miles, the two roads joined again near a market town, and before long Ivan had met the merchants once more. "Thank you for saving us from the robbers," said one of them. "We will pay for your night's lodgings."

"I'll see the host first," said Ivan when they got to the inn. Ivan found out that the inn was owned by an old man with a young wife. He remembered his master's advice. "I'll not lodge here," he said, and while the merchants settled down to a meal of roast pork, Ivan took a room in the house next door.

Now it so happened that the young wife of the old landlord was plotting with a young monk to kill her husband and take over the inn. They saw that if they did the crime that night they could pin the blame on the merchants, who were the only guests. The pair were preparing to carry out their wicked plan in an upper room of the inn where the old man was sleeping. But they did not know that Ivan, getting ready to go to bed in his room next door, could hear them through the wall. There was a missing pine knot in the wall and Ivan looked through and saw them talking.

Suddenly, the young woman saw the hole in the wall. "We

must block that hole," she said, "or someone may see us." So the monk stood hard against the hole while the wicked woman stabbed her husband to death.

Ivan saw his chance. He took his knife and cut out a piece of the monk's habit while he stood against the hole.

In the morning, the crime was discovered and the wife went screaming to the justices. "It must have been that gang of wicked merchants staying at the inn," she cried. The merchants were marched off to prison, and Ivan saw them pass.

"Woe to us, Ivan!" they cried. "Our luck is running out. We are taken for this murder, but we are all innocent."

"Tell them to find the real murderers," called Ivan.

"But no one knows who committed the crime," said one of the merchants.

"If I cannot bring them to justice," said Ivan, "let them hang *me* for the murder."

So Ivan went to the justices and told them everything he had heard. At first, the justices did not believe him, but when he showed them the piece of cloth he had cut from the monk's robe, they knew it must be true, and the young wife and the monk were arrested. The merchants were released, thanked Ivan for his trouble, and went on their way.

When Ivan got home to his wife she ran to greet him. "You come in the nick of time," she said. "I have just found a fine purse of gold. It has no name on it, but it must belong to the lord of the manor."

"Honesty is the best policy," said Ivan, remembering the third piece of advice. "Let us take it to the lord's house."

When they got to the lord's castle, they left the purse with the servant at the gatehouse.

One day, the lord passed Ivan's house, and his wife mentioned the purse to him. "I know of no purse returned to me," said the lord, in puzzlement. "Surely my servant must have kept it for himself."

Off they went to the castle and sought out the servant. As soon as the lord accused him, the servant saw that he was

found out, and gave up the purse. The lord frowned at his wicked servant. "I have no use for dishonest men. Be gone from my castle," he ordered.

Then the lord turned to Ivan. "Will you be my servant in his place?"

"Thank you," said Ivan. And he and his wife were given fine new quarters in the castle. When they were moving in, Ivan remembered the cake his old master had given him. They cut themselves a piece, and out fell three gold coins, Ivan's wages for his work for his old master. "Truly, honesty is the best policy," laughed Ivan. And his wife agreed.

Cherry of Zennor

Near the village of Zennor in Cornwall lived a man everyone called Old Honey. With him in his tiny two-room hut lived his wife and ten children. They managed with the little living space they had, and grew what food they could on the land around the hut, adding limpets and periwinkles, which they gathered from the shore.

Old Honey's favorite daughter was Cherry, who could run as fast as the wind. She was always mischievous, but had such a winning smile that everyone liked her. She loved to steal the horse of the miller's boy when he came into the village, and would ride out to the cliffs. If the miller's boy seemed to be catching up, she would leave the horse behind, and hide in the rocks or cairns that there were along the coast, and neither the miller's boy nor any other could catch her or find her.

Cherry was a sweet-natured child, but when she reached her teens she became discontented. She wanted so much to have a new dress, so that she could cut a fine figure at church or at the fair. But there was no money for dresses, so she had to mend the one she had. She thought it was not fit for her to go

to the fair and look for a sweetheart.

One day, Cherry decided that she would leave home and look for a job, so that she might have money of her own. So the next morning she wrapped her few possessions in a bundle and set off. On she trudged, but when she came to the cross roads at Lady Downs, she sat down on a stone and cried, for she felt tired, missed her family, and wished she had not set out on her own.

Just as she was drying her eyes and deciding that she would return to her family, a gentleman appeared. Cherry thought this was odd, since she had seen no one coming before, and on the Downs you could see for miles around. When the man bid her "Good morning," Cherry told him that she had left home to seek her fortune, but that she had lost heart and was going to return.

"I did not expect such good luck," said the man. "I am looking for a young woman to come and keep house for me, for I am recently a widower." So Cherry decided that she would go with the man, and they set off across the Downs together.

As they went, the gentleman told Cherry that she would have little to do but milk the cow and look after his small son. He did not live far away, he said, explaining that his home was in the "low country", the valley beyond the Downs. After a while they walked into an area where the lanes were sunk deep into the ground, with trees and bushes growing high on either side. Little sunlight reached the lane where they walked, but there was a rich scent of sweetbrier and honeysuckle, and these pleasant scents reassured Cherry, who might otherwise have been afraid of the dark.

Next they came to a river, and the gentleman picked Cherry up around the waist and carried her across. On the other side, the lane seemed even darker, and Cherry held the man's arm.

Soon they came to the gentleman's home. When she saw the place, Cherry could not believe her eyes. The dark lane had not prepared her for a place of such beauty. The garden was full of flowers of every color, fruit of all descriptions hung down from the trees, and birds sat in the branches, singing as if they were pleased that the master of the house had come home.

The garden was so unlike her own home that Cherry remembered how her grandmother had told her of places that had been enchanted by the little people. Could this be such a place?

Cherry looked up as a voice called "Papa!" and a small child, about two or three years old, came rushing towards the gentleman. But when Cherry looked at the child, although he was small, his faced seemed old and wrinkled. She was about to speak to the child when a haggard old woman appeared out of the house and came towards them.

"This is Aunt Prudence, my late wife's grandmother," said the gentleman. He explained that the old woman would stay until Cherry had learned her work, then she would leave.

When they went indoors, Cherry found that the house was even more beautiful than its garden. Aunt Prudence produced a large and tasty meal, and they all sat down to eat, after which the old woman showed Cherry to her room.

"When you are in bed, keep your eyes closed," said Aunt Prudence. "If you open your eyes, you may see things that frighten you." Then she explained what work Cherry would have to do the next day. She was to take the boy to the spring and wash him, after which she was to rub some ointment into his eyes. She would find the ointment in a box hidden in a gap in the rock by the spring. On no account should she put the ointment on her own eyes. Then she was to call the cow and milk her, and give the boy milk for his breakfast.

The following morning, Cherry rose early and began her work. She went with the little boy to the spring, where she washed him and put the ointment on his eyes. Then she looked around for the cow, but could see no beast anywhere. So Cherry made a clicking noise, which she had used when calling the cows in Zennor, and suddenly a fine cow appeared from among the trees, and Cherry sat down to milk her.

After breakfast, the old woman showed Cherry everything in

the kitchen. Then Aunt Prudence told Cherry that under no circumstances should she try to go into any of the locked rooms in the house. "You might see something that would frighten you," she repeated. After this warning, Cherry went out to help her master in the garden. She and the gentleman got on well, but Cherry did not like the old woman, who was often hovering around in the background, muttering, as if she did not like the girl and wanted her gone.

When Cherry seemed settled in her new home, Prudence said, "Now you shall see some parts of the house you have not seen before." One room had a floor that was polished like glass and around all the walls were figures of men, women, and children, all made of stone. They looked to Cherry as if they were real people who had somehow been turned to stone, and she shivered with fear as she looked at them.

Poor Cherry thought she had come into a house of wicked conjurors, and looked at the old woman in fear. "I don't want to see any more," she said.

But the old woman laughed, and pushed Cherry into another room, where she was made to polish a large box that looked like a coffin on legs. "Rub harder, harder!" shouted the old woman, with a look of madness in her eyes, and as Cherry 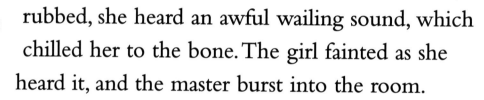 rubbed, she heard an awful wailing sound, which chilled her to the bone. The girl fainted as she heard it, and the master burst into the room.

When he saw what had happened, the gentleman threw the old woman out of the house, shouting that she should never have shown Cherry the locked room. Then he gave Cherry a soothing drink to revive her. It made Cherry feel better, and it also made her forget exactly what she had seen. But she knew that she had been frightened, and that she did not want to go into that part of the house again.

Life was much better for Cherry with the old woman gone. She was happy in her master's house, but still curious about what was going on there. One day, when her master was out, she decided to try some of the child's ointment on her own

eyes. As she rubbed in the ointment, she felt a terrible burning and dashed to the pool under the rock to splash cool water on her eyelids. As she did so, she saw hundreds of tiny people at the bottom of the pool – and among them was her master!

The ointment had given Cherry the ability to see the little people, and when she looked, she could see them everywhere, hiding in the flowers, swinging in the trees, running around under blades of grass. Another time, she saw her master playing with a host of the little people. One of them, dressed up like a queen, was dancing on top of the coffin, and the master took her in his arms and kissed her.

Next day, when Cherry and her master were together in the garden, he bent to kiss her. This was enough for Cherry. "Kiss the little people like yourself, as you do when you go under the water," she cried, and slapped her master on the face. The gentleman knew that Cherry had used some of the ointment on her eyes. She would have to leave him for good.

Sadly, Cherry and her master parted. He gave her a bundle full of clothes and other fine things, picked up a lantern, and led her away from his garden, along the sunken lanes, and towards the Downs. Then he gave the girl a final kiss, and said with a hint of sadness in his voice that he was sorry, but that

she must be punished for her curiosity. Perhaps he would see her sometimes if she walked upon the Downs.

So Cherry returned to Zennor. Her people were surprised to see her, for she had been away for so long, without sending news of her whereabouts, that they had thought she was dead. When she told her story to her parents, they could not believe it at first, and thought she was telling it to cover up some mischief that she had been part of. But Cherry insisted that her story was true, and in time her family accepted what she said. Often she wandered on the Lady Downs, looking for her old master. But she never saw him again.

Skillywidden

A man was cutting furze on Trendreen Hill one fine day, and he saw one of the little people stretched out, fast asleep, on the heath. The man took off the thick cuff that he wore at his work, crept up quietly, and popped the little man into the cuff before he could wake up. Then he carried his find home with care, and let the creature out on to the hearth stone.

When he awoke, the fairy looked quite at home and soon began to enjoy himself playing with the children. They called him Bob of the Heath, and Bob told the man that he would show him where to find crocks of gold hidden on the hillside.

Several days later, the neighbors joined together to bring away the harvest of furze, and all came to the man's house to celebrate the end of their task with a hearty meal. To hide Bob away from prying eyes, the man locked him in the barn with the children.

But the fairy and his playmates were cunning, and soon found a way out of the barn. Before long they were playing a game of dancing and hide-and-seek all around the great heap of furze in the yard.

As they played, they saw a tiny man and woman searching round the furze. "Oh my poor Skillywidden," said the tiny woman. "Where can you be? Will I ever set eyes on you again?"

"Go back indoors," said Bob to the children. "My mother and father have come looking for me. I must go back with them now." Then he cried, "Here I am mommy!" And before the children knew what had happened, their playmate Bob had vanished with his parents, and they were left in the yard.

When they told their father what had happened, the man was angry, and gave them a beating for escaping from the locked barn.

After this the furze-cutter sometimes went to Trendreen Hill to look for fairies and crocks of gold. But he was never able to find either.

Tom and the Giant Blunderbuss

Long ago, when the world was ruled by giants, there was a young giant called Tom. Although he was young and strong, Tom was a lazy lad who spent most of the time mooching around with his hands in his pockets. Now and then, Tom would spring into action, and would move dozens of massive boulders to build a wall, just to show what he could do if he tried. But usually he was idle.

Tom's mother grew sick of her son's idleness, and after much nagging, persuaded him to take a job driving a brewer's wagon. Tom thought that if he had to have a job, this would be a good one, because at least he would be able to get plenty to drink. So off he went to live in the nearest market town, where he began to work for the brewer.

One day he was out with his wagon when he came across a group of men trying to lift a fallen tree. They seemed to be making a poor effort of it, so he stopped, helped them, and in a trice had lifted the tree where they wanted it. The men thanked him, and he set off again along the road to St Ives.

After a while, Tom came to a place where a wall blocked the road. Tom knew that the lands behind the wall belonged to a great giant known as Blunderbuss. Many years before, the road had gone straight ahead, but now it was blocked by Blunderbuss's wall. If the giant had not lived there, Tom could have gone straight on in the direction of St Ives. But as it was, he would have to go a long way round.

Tom looked at the giant's gate and wondered whether he should take the short cut through. But the giant had a cruel reputation. He had married several times, and people said that he had killed each of his wives. Tom therefore thought better of trespassing on the giant's land, and carried on his journey by the normal road.

But on his way back, Tom was tired and full with the four gallons of beer he had drunk at St Ives, and he decided to take the shorter route home. So he drove his wagon through the giant's great gate and across the field where the giant's cattle grazed contentedly. When he had gone about a mile, he arrived at a gate in a high wall which surrounded the giant's castle.

The only way was forward, so Tom pushed open the gate and began to drive his oxen across the castle courtyard. As he went along, Tom heard some dogs barking loudly, and then the great giant himself emerged from his castle.

"What are you doing driving into my castle courtyard and disturbing my afternoon sleep?" roared the giant.

"I am on the right road," said Tom. "You have no right to stop me going home."

"I will not trouble myself to argue with a saucy young rascal like you," said Blunderbuss. "I shall fetch a twig and beat you to my gate."

The giant pulled up an elm tree taller than three men and **began to strip the branches from the trunk. He still seemed to** be half asleep, but he could do this without any effort at all. Tom saw what he was doing, and looked around for a weapon to defend himself. His eye lighted on his wagon, so he pulled out one of the axles, took one of the wooden wheels as a

shield, and stood ready for
the giant's blows.

Blunderbuss rushed at Tom,
but Tom dodged quickly, the
ground was slippery, and the
giant squelched into the
mud. Tom could have killed
the giant easily when he was
down, but the young lad
thought that this was unfair.
So he merely tickled
Blunderbuss in the ribs with
his axle, and said, "Up you
get. Let's have another turn."

Quickly, Blunderbuss got
up and rushed at Tom without warning. But Tom was
ready for him, and held out
his axle so that it pierced the
giant's body right through.
Blunderbuss gave out a
dreadful roar.

"Stop bleating like a sheep!"
said Tom. "I will pull out my

axle, then we can have another turn."

But when he withdrew his weapon, Tom saw that blood was pouring from the giant's wound. Tom cut some turf and gave this to the giant to plug the hole, and then Tom was ready to fight once more. But the giant Blunderbuss held up his hand. "No, I can fight no more. You have wounded me mortally. And you have done well, fighting bravely even when I tried to trick you by rushing at you when you were not prepared. I would like to do you some good, for you are the only one who has

been brave enough to stand up to me. Listen carefully. I have no near relations and I want you to have my wealth and my lands when I die. In my castle cellar, two dogs guard my gold.

The dogs are called Catchem and Tearem. If you go into the cellar they will attack you unless you call them by their names. Simply do this and you can take the gold."

Tom listened in silence as the giant told him of the wealth and lands that he would own. In the end he asked, "Did you kill your wives?"

"No. They died of natural causes. Please do not let people tell lies about me when I am dead."

And Tom was about to reassure the giant and tell him that his time was not yet come, when Blunderbuss closed his eyes, and all was over.

Tom went back home with his wagon, but returned to the giant's castle and found that all that Blunderbuss had told him was true. He also found the giant's young wife, who quickly got to know and love Tom. Soon the two were married, and they lived for many a long year in the castle by the road.

I Don't Know

Once there was a Duke who lived in Brittany, and he was riding home one day with his manservant when they saw a young child lying asleep and alone by the side of the road. The Duke was curious and sad to see a young boy, about five years old, left by the roadside, so he got down from his horse, went over to the boy, and woke him up.

"Who has left you here, my boy?" asked the Duke.

"I don't know."

"Who are your parents?"

"I don't know."

"Which town do you come form?"

"I don't know."

"What are you called?"

"I don't know."

"Well, no one seems to be taking care of you, so we will take you home and keep you safe." So the Duke took the child home to his castle, and called him N'oun-Doaré, which is the Breton for "I don't know."

N'oun-Doaré grew up in the family of the Duke and proved

to be a healthy, intelligent child. The Duke sent him to school and the lad grew into a handsome young man.

When N'oun-Doaré was eighteen, the Duke brought him back to live at the castle, and, to show N'oun-Doaré how pleased he was with his progress, took him to the local fair to buy him his own sword and his own horse.

First the Duke took N'oun-Doaré to look for a horse. There were many horse-dealers at the fair, but N'oun-Doaré could find no steed that suited him. Then they met a man leading an old mare and N'oun-Doaré shouted, "Yes! That is the horse I want!"

The Duke was surprised. "That old nag?" he said. But the boy insisted.

As the horse's owner was handing over the beast, he spoke quietly to N'oun-Doaré. "You have made a good choice, my boy. Look at these knots in the mare's mane. If you undo one of them, she will fly fifteen hundred leagues through the air."

Then the Duke and N'oun-Doaré went to see the armorer, and looked at many swords. But none was quite right for N'oun-Doaré. Then they came to a junk shop and saw an old, rusty sword. "That is the sword I would like."

"But it's an old, rusty thing," protested the Duke. "You deserve much better than that."

"Please buy it for me in any case, and I will put it to good use."

So they bought the old sword and the lad was pleased. He was even more excited when he looked closely at the weapon and saw that it had a faint inscription, almost covered by the rust. The words "I am invincible" were engraved on the sword.

When they got home, N'oun-Doaré could not wait to try a magical flight with his mare, and before long he was undoing one of the knots in her mane. Off they flew to Paris, where N'oun-Doaré marveled at the sights of the great city. It chanced that the Duke was also there, for he had been called to attend the king. When he met the boy, they went to the royal palace together. The Duke introduced N'oun-Doaré to the king, and the lad was given a job looking after some of the

royal stables.

One night, N'oun-Doaré was passing a cross roads when he saw something glinting in the moonlight. He found that it was a crown, and that it was adorned with diamonds that shone in the dark. He picked up the crown when a voice said "Be on your guard if you take it." N'oun-Doaré did not know where the voice came from, but it was actually the voice of his old mare. It made N'oun-Doaré pause, but in the end he picked up the crown and took it with him.

He told no one about the crown and kept it secretly in the stables, but two of the other servants noticed it shining through the keyhole and went to tell the king. The king took the crown and called all his wise men about him. But none of them knew where the crown had come from. There was an inscription on the crown, but it was in a strange language and none of the wise men could read it.

Then a small child spoke up, saying that the crown belonged to the Princess of the Golden Fleece. The king turned to N'oun-Doaré: "Bring me the Princess of the Golden Fleece to be my wife, otherwise you will meet your death."

So the lad got on his mare and began his search for the princess, although in truth he had little idea about where to look. As he rode, he came to a beach, and N'oun-Doaré saw a fish stuck on the sand. The creature seemed to be breathing its last. "Put it back in the sea," said the mare, and N'oun-Doaré did so.

"Great thanks to you," said the fish. "You have saved the life of the king of the fish."

A while later they came to a place where a bird was trapped in a snare. "Let the creature go," said the mare, and N'oun-Doaré did so.

"Great thanks to you," said the bird. "You have saved the life of the king of the birds."

Further along on their journey they came to a great castle and nearby a man was chained to a tree. "Set him free," said the mare, and N'oun-Doaré did so.

"Great thanks to you," said the man. "You have saved the life of the Demon King."

"Whose castle is this?" asked N'oun-Doaré.

"It is the castle of the Princess of the Golden Fleece," replied the Demon King. They had reached their goal at last.

They entered the castle and N'oun-Doaré explained why he had come. The princess was unwilling to go at first, but N'oun-Doaré tricked her on to his horse, and away they flew before she could dismount. They quickly arrived back in Paris, where the king wanted to marry without delay.

"Before I marry, I must have my own ring," said the princess.

The king asked N'oun-Doaré to bring him the ring,

and N'oun-Doaré looked about in despair. How would he find it? Then the mare whispered to him, "Ask the king of the birds, who you saved. He will help you."

So they went to the king of the birds and explained that they needed the ring. The king of the birds called all the birds to him. He chose the smallest bird of all, the wren, and told her to bring the ring to the princess. "The wren is the best bird for this task," he explained. "She will be able to fly through the keyhole of the princess's chamber."

Soon the wren returned with the ring, and the king wanted to marry straight away. But the princess had another demand. "I must have my own castle brought to me," she said.

"How shall I ever achieve this?" said N'oun-Doaré in despair.

But the mare whispered to him, "Ask the Demon King, who you saved. He will help you."

So they went to the Demon King, and he called a whole army of demons, and they set to work moving the princess's castle, bit by bit, to Paris, until her wish had come true. The king, of course, wanted to marry straight away, but the princess had a final demand. "I do not have the key to my castle, for it was dropped into the sea when we flew here to Paris on N'oun-Doaré's mare."

N'oun-Doaré saw that this was a task for the king of the fish, who called all his subjects to him. Finally, a fish arrived with

the diamond–studded key in its mouth.

At last, the Princess agreed to marry the king. When the guests arrived they were amazed to see N'oun-Doaré leading his mare into the church. When the king and princess were pronounced man and wife, the mare's skin vanished, and there stood a beautiful young woman. "Please marry me, N'oun-Doaré," she said. "I am the daughter of the king of Tartary."

N'oun-Doaré and the princess set off arm in arm to Tartary. People say they lived happily ever after there, but they were never seen in Brittany again.

The Fenoderee

On the Isle of Man lived a fairy who had been sent out of fairyland because he had had a passion for a mortal girl. The fairy folk found out about his love for the girl when he was absent from one of their gatherings. They found him dancing with his love in the merry Glen of Rushen. When the other fairies heard what he was doing, they cast a spell, forcing him to live for ever on the Isle of Man, and making him ugly and hairy. This is why people called him the Fenoderee, which means "hairy one" in the Manx language.

Although his appearance frightened people when they saw him, the Fenoderee was usually kind to humans, for he never forgot the girl he loved, and wanted to do what he could for her people. Sometimes he even helped people with their work, and used what was left of his fairy magic to carry out tasks which would have been exhausting for the strongest of men.

One thing the Fenoderee liked to do was to help the farmers in their fields. On one occasion he mowed a meadow for a farmer. But instead of being grateful, the farmer complained that the Fenoderee had not cut the grass short enough.

The Fenoderee was still sad at losing his mortal love, and angry that the farmer was so ungrateful, so next year at mowing time, he let the farmer do the job himself.

As the farmer walked along, swishing his scythe from side to side, the Fenoderee crept behind him, cutting up roots, and getting so close to the farmer that the man risked having his feet cut off.

When the farmer told this story, people knew that they should be grateful when the Fenoderee helped them with their work. So the custom arose of leaving the creature little gifts when he had been especially helpful.

On one occasion, a man was building himself a new house of stone. He found the stone he wanted on the cliffs by the beach, and paid some of the men of the parish to help him quarry it. There was one large block of fine marble which he especially wanted, but no matter how hard they tried, the block was too heavy to be moved, even if all the men of the parish tried to shift it.

Next day they were surprised to see that not only had the huge block of marble been carried to the building site, but all the other stone that the builder needed had been moved too.

At first, everyone wondered how the stone could have got there. But then someone said, "It must have been the **Fenoderee who was working for us in the night." The builder**

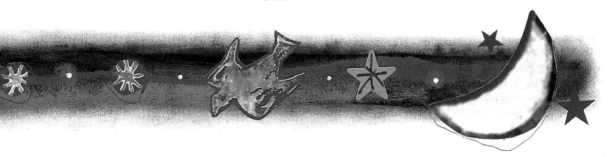

saw that this must be true, and thought that he should give the Fenoderee a handsome reward.

So he took some clothes of the right size for the creature, and left them in one of the places where he was sometimes seen. That night, the Fenoderee appeared and found the clothes. Those who watched him were surprised at his sadness as he lifted each item up in turn and said these words:

Cap for the head, alas, poor head!

Coat for the back, alas, poor back!

Breeches for the breech, alas, poor breech!

If these all be thine, thine cannot be the merry glen of Rushen.

With these words, the Fenoderee walked away, and has never been seen since in that neighbourhood.

A Bride and a Hero

Long ago the Irish believed that there was a faraway land
called Tir na n-Og, the Land of Youth. Time went much more
slowly there, and people stayed younger much longer. It was
the law in Tir na n-Og that every seven years a race was held.
All the strongest men of the land took part. The race began in
front of the royal palace and finished at the top of a hill two
miles away. At the summit of the hill was placed a chair, and
the first runner to sit on the chair became king of Tir na n-Og
for the next seven years.

There was once a king of Tir na n-Og who was worried that
he would lose his kingdom in the next race, so he sent for his
chief druid.

"How long shall I win the race and rule this land before
another reaches the chair before me?" he asked the druid.

"Have no fear," replied the druid. "You will rule for ever,
unless your own son-in-law wins the race and takes the crown
from you."

The king of Tir na n-Og had but one daughter, Niamh, and
as yet she was not married. So the king decided that he would

keep his kingdom by making his daughter so ugly that no man
would marry her. He borrowed his druid's staff, and struck the
girl with it, and a pig's head appeared on her shoulders.

When the druid heard what had happened, he was very sorry
that he had told the king to beware his son-in-law. He went to
Niamh to talk to her.

"Shall I always be like this?" said Niamh to the druid.

"Yes," replied the druid. "You will always look like this unless
you go to Ireland and marry one of the sons of Fin."

So Niamh set out for Ireland, hoping to meet one of Fin's
sons, and wondering how she could persuade him to marry
her. When Niamh had been in Ireland for a while she saw a

handsome young man called Oisin, and she was overjoyed when she found out that his father was Fin himself.

It happened one day that Oisin was out hunting, and he and his men hunted further afield, and killed more game than they had ever done before. When Oisin turned to go home, his men were exhausted and hungry, and could carry none of the game home with them, so Oisin was left with his three dogs and a great pile of carcasses.

When the men left Oisin alone, Niamh went up to him and watched him looking at the game. When he saw her approach, the young man said "I shall be sorry to

leave behind some of the meat I have killed today."

"If you tie some of the game in a bundle, I will help you carry it," said Niamh. And off they walked together.

When they had talked for a while, it was clear to Oisin that Niamh was a fine young woman, caring and kind, and it struck the lad that she would probably be attractive too, if she did not have a pig's head on her shoulders. So Oisin asked her about the pig's head, and Niamh explained how she had been told that the only way to get back her own head was to come to Ireland marry one of the sons of Fin.

Oisin smiled. "If that is all it takes for you to get back your

beauty, then you shall not have a pig's head for long," he said.

So it was that Niamh married Oisin, son of Fin. As soon as the ceremony was over, the pig's head vanished, and Niamh's own beautiful face was revealed to her husband. And when he saw Niamh in her new beauty, he loved her deeply.

Soon it was clear that Niamh longed to return to the land of Tir na n-Og, and when she told Oisin of her wish, he was keen to go there with her. He knew that it was the land where people never grow old, and if he went there he would be young for ever. When they arrived at the castle of Niamh's

father, there was great celebration, for everyone had thought that the princess was lost for ever. So for a while the king lived happily with his daughter and son-in-law.

But after a while it was the time for the seven-yearly race to find who should be king. All the likely men in the kingdom, including the king and Oisin, gathered for the race. And before any other competitor was half way up the hill, Oisin was sitting in the seat at the top. No one could deny that it was Oisin's right to be king of Tir na n-Og.

Oisin ruled the Land of Youth for many years, and no one ever argued with his right to be king. He loved his wife dearly, and they were always seen together—in the palace, in the town, or riding their swift grey horse together. Oisin marveled that he kept his youth, just as did anyone who had been born in Tir na n-Og and lived there all their years. But there was one sadness. Oisin missed his Irish homeland and longed to go back for a visit. He spoke of his wish to Niamh and she turned to him with a warning. "It will be dangerous for you if you return to Ireland," she said. "If you set foot on your native soil, you will lose your youth. You will become a blind old man and you will never come home to me."

Oisin could not believe that this would happen so easily.

"How long do you think you have lived with me in Tir na n–Og?" she asked.

"About three years," replied Oisin.

"But three of our years are like three hundred in Ireland."

Nothing that Niamh could say could change Oisin's mind. He insisted that he wanted to go back. So Niamh decided to help him, in the hope that her husband could hold on to his youth. "Ride to Ireland and do not dismount," she said. "You will only lose your youth if you put your own foot on Irish soil. But if you leave the saddle, the steed will come back to Tir na n-Og and you will be left, old and blind, in Ireland."

With this warning ringing in his ears, Oisin set off for his homeland. The beautiful white horse carried him across both land and sea, and he came at last to Ireland. It was rainy and

windy, but Oisin was happy to be home once more.

Soon he passed a girl and he asked her where he might find the house of Fin and his family. For the land and the buildings seemed changed from when Oisin had last been there. The girl looked at him with a puzzled expression. "I know of no such people," she said. "They do not live around here." And yet Oisin was sure that he was in the right neighborhood.

He passed other people on his way, and asked each one about Fin and his household of mighty warriors. But no one seemed to know who he was talking about—which was strange, since Fin and his men had been among the most famous in Ireland.

Finally Oisin asked an old man if he knew the whereabouts

of Fin. "I remember my old grandfather talking about Fin and his warriors," said the old man. "They lived in these parts about three hundred years ago."

So Oisin's father and all his family were dead. Oisin could still not believe it. He found the fortress Fin had built, but it was in ruins. He began to believe that what the old man said was true, and that three years in the Land of Youth really were the same as three hundred mortal years.

Oisin decided to seek out the High King of Ireland himself, to tell him of his adventure. As he was riding along the road,

he came across a group of men who were trying to lift a stone. Since he had arrived in Ireland, Fin had noticed that the men seemed weak and feeble compared with those in Tir na n-Og, and these men were no exception. Six of them were tugging away at the stone, but they could not shift it, let alone lift it up into the cart that stood waiting nearby.

Riding up to the men, Oisin called that he would help them. He leaned over to pick up the stone and threw it into the cart, but the effort put Oisin off balance. As he reached out to stop himself falling, one of the stirrups broke and the hero tumbled off his horse and landed on the floor.

As he fell, all the warnings of Niamh ran through his mind. And when he picked himself up from the ground he knew that it was true, he was old, stiff, and blind. He heard Niamh's horse trotting away, and knew that he would never return to the land of Tir na n-Og.

It happened that Saint Patrick lived nearby, and the holy man heard of what had happened. Soon Oisin was brought to Patrick, who gave him a room in his own house, and asked his cook to bring him food every day.

Oisin told Patrick all about his adventures, relating stories about his father Fin and his band of warriors, as well as his adventures in the land of youth, while the holy man listened patiently. Although he was old and blind, Oisin still had a little of his former strength, and sometimes, if Patrick prayed devoutly, Oisin would regain enough energy to help the Saint build his church, and to help rid Patrick of a monster that came to destroy the building before it was finished. But Oisin's strength never lasted long, and soon he would be a weak old man again and it was all he could do to eat the food brought to him by Patrick's cook. And so, old and blind, Oisin lived out the last of his days, with only his memories of Tir na n-Og to console him.

The Lazy Beauty

Once upon a time there was a poor widow who had one daughter. The mother was the most hard-working of women. Her house was neat and clean, and she was especially good at using her spinning wheel to make the finest linen thread.

The daughter was a fine-looking girl, but the laziest creature in the town. She got up late every day, spent hours eating her breakfast, and dawdled around the house doing nothing all day. Whenever she tried to cook, she burned herself, and if she did any other work, she would straight away knock something over or break one of her mother's pots. The girl even drawled her speech, as if it took too much energy to get the words out of her mouth.

One day the widow was giving her daughter a good telling off when she heard the sound of hoofbeats on the road. It was the king's son riding by. When he heard the woman's voice he stopped to talk to her.

"What is the matter? Is your child so bad that you need to scold her so?"

"Oh no, your majesty," replied the old woman, for she saw a

chance to get rid of the girl. "I was telling my daughter that she works much too hard. Do you know, my lord, she can spin three whole pounds of flax in a single day? Then the next day, she will weave it into good linen cloth, and sew it all into shirts the following day!"

The prince reflected when he heard what the woman had to say. "That is amazing," he said. "Surely my mother, herself a great spinner, would be pleased with your daughter. Tell her to put her bonnet on and come with me. We might even make a fine princess of her, if she herself would like that."

The two women were thrown into confusion. Neither of them could have imagined that the old woman's trick would

have worked so well. But quickly enough, the girl had her outdoor clothes on and was lifted up to ride behind the prince. His majesty gave the mother a bulging purse in exchange for her daughter, and off they rode in the direction of the palace.

Now the girl did not know what to do. But it seemed to her that doing little and saying little had served her well to this day, so when she got to the palace she answered briefly and said but few words, in the hope that she would not show herself up as a lazy idiot.

By the evening, she and the prince seemed to be getting on well and the time came for them to show the girl her room. As she opened the door the queen showed her the work she was to do in the morning. "Here are three pounds of good flax. You may begin as soon as you like in the morning, and I shall expect to see them turned into thread by the end of the day."

The poor girl burst into tears as the queen closed the door behind her. She regretted now that she had not listened to everything her mother had told her about spinning, and that she had not taken all the opportunities she had had to learn the craft. She slept little that night with worry and vexation.

When the morning finally came, there was the great wooden spinning wheel waiting for her, and the girl started to spin. But her thread kept breaking, and one moment it was thick, the

next it was thin. She burst into tears as the thread broke again.

At that very moment, a little old woman with big feet appeared in the room. "What is the matter, my fair maiden?" asked the woman.

"I have all this flax to spin, and whatever I do, the thread seems to break," said the girl.

"Ah, if you invite the old woman with the big feet to your wedding with the prince, I will spin your thread for you," the woman offered.

"I will be glad for you to come to the wedding if you will do this work for me," said the girl. "I shall honor you for as long as I live."

"Very well. Stay in your room until evening, and tell the queen that her thread will be ready tomorrow," said the old woman.

And it was all as the old woman had said. The queen came, saw the beautiful thread, and told the girl to rest. "Tomorrow I shall bring you my fine wooden loom, and you can turn all this thread into cloth," she promised.

Of course, this made the girl more frightened than ever, for she was no better a weaver than a spinner. She sat in her room, trembling, waiting for the loom to be brought to her. When the loom was brought, she sat at it and cried once more.

Suddenly, another old woman appeared in the room, a woman with great hips and a small voice, and she asked why the girl was crying.

"I have all this thread to weave, but I cannot work the loom," said the girl.

"Ah, if you invite the old woman with the big hips to your wedding with the prince, I will weave your cloth for you," the woman offered.

"I will be glad for you to come to the wedding if you will do this work for me," said the girl. "I shall honor you for as long as I live."

"Very well. Stay in your room until evening, and tell the queen that her cloth will be ready tomorrow."

Once more, the work was done and the queen was pleased with the cloth. But this time, the girl found herself with the task of sewing the cloth into shirts for the prince. The girl was now in deep despair. She was so close to marrying the prince, but she had no skill whatsoever with the needle. As she sat and cried a third old woman, with a big red nose, appeared in her room. The girl explained her plight.

"Ah, if you invite the old woman with the red nose to your wedding with the prince, I will sew your shirts for you," the woman offered.

"I will be glad for you to come to the wedding if you will do this work for me," said the girl. "I shall honor

you for as long as I live."

"Very well. Stay in your room until evening, and tell the queen that the shirts will be ready tomorrow."

So again the work was done, the queen was pleased, and the girl found that preparations for the wedding were being made.

When the wedding came, it was the most lavish feast anyone could remember. The girl's old mother was invited, and the queen kept talking to her about how her daughter would enjoy herself spinning, weaving, and sewing after the honeymoon. Just as she was talking about this, the footman approached the high table and announced another guest. "The princess's aunt, Old Woman Big-foot, has arrived." The girl blushed, but the prince seemed to happy for her to come in. "Tell her that she is welcome, and find a place for her," said the prince.

When someone asked the old woman why her feet were so big, she explained that it was from standing all day working at the spinning wheel.

"Why, my dear," said the prince. "I shall never let you stand all day spinning."

Soon the second old woman arrived at the feast. When she was asked why her hips were so great, she said it came from sitting all day at the loom.

"Why my dear," said the prince. "I shall never let you sit all day weaving."

Finally the third old woman took her place. She explained that her nose had grown big and red from bending down sewing, so that the blood ran always to her nose.

"Why, my dear," said the prince. "I shall never let you sit all day sewing."

So it came about that the lazy beauty never had to spin, or weave, or sew again, and she lived happily in her laziness at the prince's court.

Paddy O'Kelly and the Weasel

There was once a man called Paddy O'Kelly, and he lived in County Galway. Paddy had an old donkey that he wanted to sell, so he got up early one morning and began the journey to market. He hoped one day to be able to buy a horse, though he knew he would not get enough money for the donkey to buy himself a fine steed that day.

Paddy had gone a few miles when it started to rain, so he decided to shelter in a large house. No one seemed to be around, so he went into a room with a fire blazing in the grate. After a while he saw a big weasel come into the room and put something yellow on the grate; then the creature ran away. Soon afterwards, the weasel reappeared, went to the grate, and put down another yellow object. Paddy O'Kelly could see now that these yellow objects were gold coins, and he watched as the weasel came back and forth, every time leaving a guinea on the grate.

When the weasel seemed to stop bringing the coins, Paddy got up, scooped them into his pocket, and went on his way.

But he had not gone far when the weasel ran up to him, screeching and jumping up at him. Paddy tried to beat her off with a stick, but she clung on until some passing men let loose their dog, which chased her away. In the end, she disappeared down a hole in the ground.

Paddy sold his donkey at the market, and used some of the weasel's gold to buy himself a fine horse. He was returning home the way he had come when the weasel popped up out of her hole and attacked the horse. The steed bolted, and ended up nearly drowning in a nearby ditch, until two men passing by helped him pull the beast out. Paddy was exhausted when he got home, so he tethered the horse in the cowshed and went straight to bed.

Next morning, when he went to feed the horse, he saw the weasel running out of the cowshed. The creature had blood on her fur, and Paddy feared the worst. Sure enough, when he got to the shed he found not only his horse, but two cows and two calves dead on the floor.

Paddy called his dog and gave chase, and soon they were catching up the weasel. Suddenly, the creature ran inside a small hovel by the side of the road, closely followed by the dog, which started barking. When Paddy pushed open the door, there was no weasel to be seen, but an old woman sat on a chair in the corner.

"Did you see a weasel coming in, at all?" asked Paddy.

"I did not," said the old woman.

But the dog's instinct was to carry on the hunt, and he leapt at the old woman's throat, making her screech with a noise just like the weasel's cry. Paddy O'Kelly saw that woman and weasel were one and the same.

"Call off your dog and I'll make you rich!" said the woman.

The old woman explained that long ago she had committed a great crime. Her sin would be forgiven if Paddy took twenty pounds to the church to pay for a hundred and sixty masses to be said for her. She told Paddy that if he dug beneath a bush in a nearby field, he would find a pot filled with gold. He could pay for the masses with the money, and use what was left over to buy the big old house where first he saw the weasel.

"Do not be afraid if you see a big black dog coming out of the money pot," she warned. "He is a son of mine and will do you no harm. Soon I will die, and when I die, please do one thing more for me. Light a fire in this hut and burn it and my body together."

Straightaway Paddy went to the bush, dug a hole, and found the pot of gold. As he lifted the lid from the pot, a black dog jumped out, and Paddy remembered the old woman's warning.

347

When he had the money, Paddy replaced his dead cows and horse, and also bought a flock of sheep. He called on the priest to arrange masses to be said for the old woman. And he went to see the man who owned the house where he had first seen the weasel. The owner warned Paddy that the house was haunted, but Paddy insisted on buying it, and stayed in the house all night, until a little man appeared.

The little man, whose name was Donal, made friends with

Paddy. They drank together and Donal played the bagpipes. Donal soon revealed that he was the son of the old woman, and told Paddy that he would be a good friend to him, so long as Paddy told no one else who he was.

Then Donal said, "Tonight I am visiting the Fortress of the Fairies of Connacht. Will you come with me? You shall ride there on a horse provided by me."

Paddy agreed, and at midnight, the two flew through the air on broomsticks that Donal brought with him. When they arrived, the fairy who seemed to be the leader said, "Tonight we are going to visit the high king and queen of the fairies." They seemed eager for Donal and Paddy to go with them, so off they all went.

When they arrived at the hill where the high king and queen of the fairies lived, the hillside opened up for them, and they walked inside. When all the fairies were assembled there, the king explained why they were all gathered together. "Tonight we are to play a great hurling match against the fairies of Munster. The Munster fairy folk always have two mortals to help them, so we would like you to come with us." They set off to the place where they were to play, and the fairies of

Munster were already gathered before them. And so, to the accompaniment of bagpipe music, they began their game.

Paddy saw that the Munster fairies were gaining the upper hand, so he helped the little people of Connacht, turning one of the opponents' human helpers on his back. Once this had happened, the two sides started to fight, and before long the Connacht side were the winners. The disappointed Munster fairies turned themselves into flying beetles and began to eat up all the leaves from the trees and bushes. This went on until the countryside looked quite bare, when thousands of doves flew up and devoured the beetles.

Meanwhile the Connacht fairies returned to their hill, and their chief gave Paddy a purse of gold for his help. Donal took him back home, and he was back in his bed before his wife had noticed that he had gone.

A month went past and Paddy settled down to enjoy his riches, when Donal came to Paddy and told him that his mother was dead. Paddy went to her hut and set fire to it with her body inside, just as she had asked. Once it was burned to the ground, Donal gave Paddy another purse of gold, saying, "This is a purse that will never be empty in your lifetime. I am going away now, but whenever you take money from this purse, remember me and the weasel."

Then Donal was gone, and Paddy and his wife lived long and wealthy, and left much money and a farm to their children. They all did as Donal had asked, and whenever they spent some of his mother's gold, they spared a thought for him and the weasel who had led Paddy to his wealth, when he had gone to sell his old donkey long ago.

The Dream of Owen O'Mulready

Owen O'Mulready was a happy man. He lived with his wife Margaret in a pleasant little house with a large garden. They had enough space to grow all the vegetables they needed, and Owen's master was kind and paid him good wages. Owen had everything he wanted out of his life—except for one thing. Owen had never had a dream. He was fascinated by the tales people told him of their dreams, and he very much wanted to have a dream of his own.

One day, Owen was digging his potatoes when his master came up and started to talk to Owen, as he often did. They began to talk about dreams, and Owen admitted that he had never had a dream, and that he would dearly like to have one.

"I can tell you how to make yourself have a dream," said Owen's master. "Before bedtime tonight, clear the fire from your hearth and make your bed in the fireplace. Sleep there tonight, and surely you will soon have a dream that you will remember for a long while, mark my words."

Owen said he would do this, and when evening came, he

cleared away the fire and made his bed in the hearth, just as his master had told him. When Margaret saw him doing this, she thought her husband had gone mad. But when he explained what his master had said, she let him do what he wanted, for she knew how badly Owen wanted his dream.

So Owen got into his hearth-bed, and soon was asleep. He had not been sleeping for long when there was a loud knock at the door. Owen opened it and a stranger was there. "I have a letter from the master which must be taken to America."

"You've arrived late for such a message," replied Owen. But he accepted the message, put on his boots, and off he went, striding towards the west.

He came to the foot of a mountain, where he met a young lad herding cows. The boy seemed to recognize him, even though Owen had not seen him before. "Where are you going in the middle of the night?" asked the boy.

"I have a letter from my master to take to America. Is this the right way?"

"Yes it is. Keep going westwards. But how will you travel across the water?"

"I will work that out in good time," said Owen. And on he went, until he came to the sea.

Owen found a crane standing on one foot by the shore.

"Good evening, Owen O'Mulready," said the crane, who, like the cow-boy, seemed to know Owen. "What are you doing here?"

Owen explained his business and said that he was puzzled about how to get over the water.

"Sit up on my back, and I will ferry you to the other side," said the crane.

"And what if you get tired before we arrive?" asked Owen.

The crane assured Owen that he would not get tired, and off they went.

They had not flown for long, when the crane started to tire. "Get off my back, Owen, for I begin to tire," said the bird.

"I can't get down now, I'll drown in the water," said Owen.

Owen began to panic, when he saw some men threshing above his head. He shouted to one of the threshers: "Thresher, reach down your flail so that I can hold on to it and give the bird a rest."

The man held down his flail and Owen clung on to it with all his strength. As soon as his weight was off the bird's back, the crane flew off with a mocking cry, leaving Owen hanging in the air.

"Bad luck to you!" Owen shouted at the bird as it vanished into the distance.

Owen's troubles were not over. The thresher began to shout

for his flail. "Let go of my flail, Owen O'Mulready. I cannot get on with my work." Owen protested, saying that he would fall into the sea and drown if he let go, but the man still shouted for his flail, and began to shake the other end, as if trying to make Owen slip off into the water.

Suddenly Owen saw a chance of rescue. A ship had appeared on the horizon, and Owen began to shout and wave with his free hand. Gradually the ship steered towards Owen and still the flail was shaking and Owen thought he might not be able to hang on long enough.

"Are we under you yet?" shouted one of the sailors on board the ship.

"Not quite," replied Owen. The ship came nearer, and the captain began to shout to Owen.

"Throw down one of your boots. If it lands on deck, we shall know we are under you."

Owen kicked one foot, and his boot fell towards the ship. But Owen did not see where it landed.

He was distracted by a terrible scream, and suddenly he heard his wife's voice shouting "Who is killing me? Owen, where can you be?"

"Is that you, Margaret?" asked Owen, not quite sure where he was, or how she had got there.

"Of course it's me," replied Margaret.

Margaret got out of bed and lit the candle. The bed was in a mess and soot was all over the sheets. At first, she could not see her husband, but found him, halfway up the chimney, climbing up and clinging on with his hands. He had on one boot, and Margaret saw that the other had come off and had hit her and woken her.

"So the master was right about your dream," said Margaret, smiling.

"Yes, he was right enough," said Owen.

And Owen O'Mulready never wanted to have another dream again.

The King and the Laborer

A laborer was digging a drain when the king came up to him and began to speak: "Are you busy at your work?"

"I am, your majesty"

"Have you a daughter?"

"I have one daughter and she is twelve years old."

"I shall ask you one question," said the king.

"I am no good at solving questions," said the laborer.

"I shall ask anyway," replied the king. "How long will it take me to travel around the world? Have your answer ready by twelve o'clock tomorrow."

The laborer wracked his brains, but he could think of no way to answer the question. When he got home, his daughter saw that he looked troubled. She asked her father what was the matter, and he told her about the king's question.

"That is not so difficult," she said. "Tell the king that if he sits on the sun or the moon it will take him twenty-four hours."

At twelve o'clock the next day, the king arrived.

"Have you the answer to my question?"

"If you sit on the moon or the sun, your majesty, it will take twenty-four hours."

The king was impressed with the laborer's answer, but sensed that he had not thought it up for himself. The man said that his daughter had told him what to say.

"Here is another question," said the king. "What is the distance between the earth and the sky?"

The laborer could not imagine how anyone could know the answer. So again, he asked his daughter, and she told her father what to do. "Take two pins and wait for the king. When he asks you what you are doing, tell him that you are going to measure the distance from the earth to the sky, but that he must buy you a long enough line, so that you can

make the measurement.

When the king arrived at twelve the next day, the man did as his daughter had suggested.

"That is a good answer," smiled the king. "I do not think that you thought of it by yourself." Again, the man admitted that his daughter had thought of the answer.

"I am impressed with your daughter," said the king. "She must come to my palace to work. If you allow it, I shall be a good friend to you."

So the laborer's daughter went to the royal palace and worked in the kitchens. She worked hard, the king was pleased

with her work, and the girl grew into a tall and beautiful young woman. But because she came from a poor family, the other servants looked down on her and teased her. When the king heard of this, he made her father a knight.

The girl could not believe the king's generosity, but it soon became clear that the king loved the girl and eventually the two were married. Afterwards, the king took his wife to one side and told her that he had something important to say.

"The queen must never speak against the king in any judgment," he warned. "If you do, you must leave the palace."

"It would not be right for me to disagree with you," said the girl. "But if you ever have cause to send me away, please grant me three armfuls of whatever I choose."

"I agree to that," said the king.

And so the king and queen began a happy married life. They soon had a son, which made them even happier, and the laborer still could not believe his luck in being made a knight. One day one of the king's tenants came to the king to complain to him. He had a mare that had foaled, but the foal was always following his neighbor's old white horse, and the man thought that his neighbor was trying to steal the foal. The neighbor, for his part, insisted that the foal was his.

"This is how to solve the question," said the king. "Put the two horses and the foal together near a gap in the wall. Then lead out each horse in turn and see which the foal follows. Whichever horse it follows, her owner shall have the foal."

The king's order was carried out, and the foal followed the old white horse.

When the queen heard what had happened, she went to the wronged owner and told him what to do. "I must not speak against the king's judgment," she said. "But go out and plant some boiled peas near where the king passes. When he asks you if you think they will grow, you can say: 'They're as likely to grow as that old white horse should give birth to a foal.'"

The man did what the queen suggested, and the king saw that he had been wronged. But he also guessed that such a clever ruse had begun with his wife. "Come here, wife," he said. "You are to leave the palace today, for you have given judgment against me."

"It is true that I did so, and I see that I must go," said the queen. "But grant me the three armfuls that I asked for."

The king was angry with her, but there was no going back on his word, so he indicated that she could take what she wanted. His anger turned to astonishment when she picked up both him and his royal throne and carried him outside the door. "That is my first armful," she said. Next, she took the young prince in her arms, carried him outside, and placed him in the king's lap. "That is my second." Finally, she gathered up an armful of all the royal charters and placed them with the prince. "And that is my third. I am happy to leave if these go with me."

The king saw that there was no parting with a woman of such wit. "Oh, dearest of women, stay with me!" he said. They went back into the palace together, and the king ordered that the foal should be returned to its rightful owner.

The Black Lad
MacCrimmon

There was once a young man called the Black Lad
MacCrimmon. He was the youngest of three brothers and he
was the most downtrodden of the three. His elder brothers
were always favored by their father, and were always given
more food, and allowed more enjoyment, than the Black Lad.
The Black Lad, on the other hand, was always given the
hardest jobs to do when the four were working together.

The father and the elder brothers were all great pipers, and
they had a fine set of pipes that they liked to play. The Black
Lad would have liked to have played the pipes too, but he was
never allowed. Always the brothers took up too much time
with their playing to give the young lad a chance.

In those days, people said that the greatest musicians of all
were the fairy folk. The Black Lad hoped that one day he
would meet one of the little people and they would teach him
to master the pipes.

The day came that the lad's father and his two brothers were
getting ready to go to the fair. The Black Lad wanted to go

too, but they would not take him. So the lad stayed at home, and when they were gone, he decided to take up the chanter from the set of pipes and see if he could play a tune.

After a while of practising, the lad began to pick out a tune on the chanter. He was starting to enjoy himself, and was so absorbed in what he was doing that he did not notice that someone was watching him and listening.

Suddenly a voice spoke in his ear: "You are doing well with your music, lad." It was none other than the Banshee from the castle.

"Which would you prefer," continued the Banshee. "Skill without success or success without skill?"

The lad replied that what he wanted most of all was skill, it did not matter about success. The Banshee smiled, as if she approved of the answer, and pulled a long hair from her head. This she wound around the reed of the chanter. Then she turned to the Black Lad MacCrimmon. "Now put your fingers on the holes of the chanter, and I will place my fingers over yours. I will guide you. When I lift one of my fingers, you lift yours that is beneath it. Think of a tune that you would like to play, and I will help you play. And my skill will rub off on you."

So the lad began to play, guided by the Banshee as she had told him. Soon he was playing with great skill, and he could master any tune that he thought of.

"Indeed you are the King of the Pipers," said the Banshee. "There has been none better before you, and none better shall come after." And with this blessing, the Banshee went on her way back to the castle.

The Black Lad carried on playing when she had left, and he could play all the tunes that he tried. When his father and

brothers returned, they could
hear him playing as they came
along the road, but by the time
they entered the house, the lad
had put away the pipes, and was
acting as if nothing at all had
happened.

None of them mentioned that
they had heard music when they
came in, but the lad's father took
down the pipes, and played as
usual. Then he handed them to
his first son, who played and passed them to the second son.
But instead of putting the pipes away after his second son had
played, old MacCrimmon handed the pipes to his youngest
son. "Now take the pipes, for no longer shall you spend all day
doing the hardest of the work and eating the meanest of the
food."

When the lad played, they heard that he was far better than
any of them. "There is no longer any point in our playing,"
said the father to the two eldest sons. "The lad is truly King of
the Pipers." And the lad's brothers knew that what their father
said was true.

Making a Wife

In the village of New Abbey lived a man called Alexander Harg, and he was newly married. His wife was a fine-looking young woman, and some people thought that if the fairies got hold of her, they would kidnap her, so great was her beauty.

A little while after his marriage, Alexander was out on the shore fishing with his net. Nearby were two old boats, left stranded on the rocks. He did not go too near for he had heard stories of little people being heard around them.

Sure enough, before long, Alexander heard a noise coming from one of the boats as if people were using hammers and chisels in there. Then a ghostly voice spoke up from the other old boat: "What are you doing in there?"

"Making a wife for Alexander Harg," came the reply.

Alexander, astounded and terrified by what he had heard, thought of nothing but running back home to see if his wife was safe. He burst through the door, locked it behind him, and took his young wife in his arms. Then he went round closing all the windows and making sure that no one could get in.

At midnight there came a loud banging at the door. The wife got up to open it. "Do not open the door," whispered Alexander. "There are strange things afoot this night."

So they sat together quietly, and after a while the knocking stopped. But just as they were relaxing again, the animals began to make terrifying bloodcurdling noises. The pair of them stayed indoors, and did not open the door until morning.

When they did so, they found a statue, carved in oak, in the shape and likeness of Alexander's wife. The good man made a bonfire and burned the effigy, and hoped never to hear the ghostly voices again.

The Missing Kettle

There was a woman who lived on the island of Sanntraigh, and she had only a kettle to hang over the fire to boil her water and cook her food. Every day one of the fairy folk would come to take the kettle. She would slip into the house quietly without saying a word, and grab hold of the kettle handle.

Each time this happened, the kettle handle made a clanking noise and the woman looked up and recited this rhyme:

> A smith is able to make
>
> Cold iron hot with coal.
>
> The due of a kettle is bones,
>
> And to bring it back again whole.

Then the fairy would fly away with the kettle and the woman would not see it again until later in the day, when the fairy brought it back, filled with flesh and bones.

There came at last a day when the woman had to leave home and go on the ferry across to the mainland. She turned to her husband, who was making a rope of heather to keep the thatch on the roof. "Will you say the rhyme that I say when the fairy comes for the kettle?" Her husband said that he would recite the rhyme just as she did, and went back to his work.

After the woman had left to catch the boat, the fairy arrived as usual, and the husband saw her come to the door. When he saw her he started to feel afraid, for unlike his wife he had had no contact with the little people. "If I lock the cottage door," he reasoned to himself, "she will go away and leave the kettle, and it will be just as if she had never come." So the husband locked the door and did not open it when the fairy tried to come in.

But instead of going away, the fairy flew up to the hole in the roof where the smoke from the fire escaped, and before the husband knew what was happening, the creature had made the kettle jump right up and out of the

hole. The fairy made away with the kettle before he knew what to do.

When his wife returned that evening, there was no kettle to be seen.

"What have you done with my kettle?" asked the woman.

"I've done nothing with it," said the husband. "But I took fright when the fairy came, closed the door to her, she took the kettle through the roof, and now it is gone."

"You pathetic wretch! Can't you even mind the kettle when I go out for the day?"

The husband tried to tell his wife that the fairy might return the kettle the next day, but the woman would hear nothing of it. Off she went straight away to the knoll where the fairies lived, to see if she could get back the kettle herself.

It was quite dark when she reached the fairies' knoll. The hillside opened to her and when she went in she saw only an old fairy sitting in the corner. The woman supposed that the others were out at their nightly mischief. Soon she found her kettle, and noticed that it still contained the remains of the food the little people had cooked in it.

She picked up the kettle and ran back down the lane, when she heard the sound of dogs chasing her. The old fairy must have let them loose. Thinking quickly, she took out some of the food from the kettle, threw it to the dogs, and hurried on.

This slowed down the dogs, and when they began to catch her up again, she threw down more food. Finally, when she got near her own gate, she poured out the rest of the food, hoping that the dogs would not come into her own house. Then she ran inside and closed the door.

Every day after that the woman watched for the fairy coming to take her kettle. But the little creature never came again.

The Saint and God's Creatures

Long ago, at the time when the first Christians were building their churches in Wales, there lived a young lad called Baglan. He worked for an old holy man, who was struck by the boy's kindness, and his eagerness to serve God.

One day it was cold and the holy man wanted a fire in his room. So he asked Baglan to move some hot coals to make a fire and to his surprise, the boy carried in some red-hot coals in the fabric of his cloak. When the boy had set the coals in the fire, not a bit of his cloak was burned or even singed.

The old holy man knew a miracle when he saw one. "You are meant to do great works for God," said the holy man. "The time is passed when you should stay here serving me." And the old man produced a crook with a shining brass handle and offered it to the lad. "Take this crook, and set off on a journey. The crook will lead your steps to a place where you must build a church. Look out for a tree which bears three different kinds of fruit. Then you will know that you have come to the right spot."

374

So the young man took the crook and walked southwards a long way. In time Baglan came to a tree. Around the roots of the tree a family of pigs were grubbing for food. In the tree's trunk had nested a colony of bees. And in the branches of the tree was a nest where a pair of crows were feeding their young.

Baglan sensed that this must be the right place. But the tree grew on sloping land, which did not seem good for building. So the young man looked around until he found a nearby area which was flat, and there he began to build his church.

He worked hard on the first day, digging the foundations, and building the first walls, and he slept well after his labors. But in the morning he was dismayed to see that the walls had all fallen down and water was seeping into the foundation

trenches. So the next day, he worked still harder, and raised the walls stronger and higher than before. But when Baglan awoke the next morning, again the walls had been flattened. He tried once more, putting still greater effort into making his building strong. But again the walls were laid low, and Baglan began to despair of ever finishing his church.

Baglan kneeled down to pray, and then he sat down to think. Perhaps he was not building in exactly the right place. So he moved his site nearer the tree, for the holy man had told him to build where he found the tree with three fruits. Straight

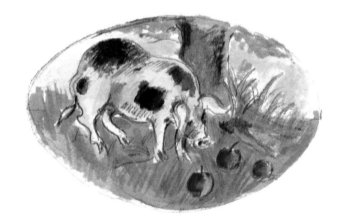

away things began to go better. The pigs, rooting with their snouts, helped him dig out the new foundations. The bees gave him honey. Even the crows offered him crusts of bread that they had scavenged. And this time, Baglan's work was lasting.

So he built and built until his walls surrounded the old tree, leaving windows for the pigs and bees, and a hole in the roof for the birds to fly in and out. As a result, his church looked

rather unusual, but he knew that it was right.

The young man kneeled down and prayed to God in thanks. And when he finished his prayer, he saw that all the animals—the pigs, and the bees, and the crows—had also fallen still and silent, as if they too, were thanking God that the work was completed.

After that, Baglan was always kind to the animals, and taught others to show kindness to them also. His crook may have been a holy relic that guided him to the tree, but even it could be used to scratch the back of the great boar.

Jamie Freel

Jamie Freel's mother was a widow, and they had little money to spare. But Jamie was one of the most hard-working lads in his village, and had a strong pair of arms, so they usually had enough to eat. Every Saturday when Jamie came home, he gave his mother all his wages, and thanked her sincerely when she returned half a penny so that he could buy his tobacco.

A short distance from where Jamie and his mother lived was an old ruined castle. The local people said that this was where the little people lived, and Jamie knew that this was true. He himself had seen them, usually at Halloween, when all the windows of the old ruin lit up, and he could hear their music inside the thick stone walls.

The more he listened to the fairy revels, the more fascinated Jamie became. So the next time Halloween came round, he decided to go to the castle, peer through the window, and see what was going on at close quarters.

When the night came, Jamie took up his cap and called to his mother, "I'm just away up to the castle, to see what is going on there tonight."

"Oh Jamie! You don't want to be risking your skin going there," said his mother. "You are all the sons I have got and I don't want to lose you to the little people."

"Have no fear, mother," he called out, making for the castle.

When Jamie looked through one of the castle windows, little people began to notice him, and he was surprised to hear them calling him by name. "Welcome, Jamie Freel, welcome! Come in and join our revels!" they called. And another of their number cried, "We're off to Dublin tonight to steal a young lady. Will you come along with us?"

Jamie liked the sound of this adventure, and was soon flying

through the air at alarming speed with the fairy host. Each town they passed, one of the little people called out its name, and soon the fairy was calling "Dublin!" and they were coming to land in a grand square in the centre of the city. Before long the fairies had kidnapped a young woman and carried her all the way back home.

Now Jamie was a good-natured lad, and the more he thought about this scheme, the more he was anxious for the feelings of the young lady. So when they were near home, he turned to one of the leaders and said, "You have all had a turn at carrying the lady, please let me carry her now." So it was Jamie who was carrying the girl when they arrived home, and he quickly put her down at his mother's door.

When it became clear that Jamie was going to keep the young woman for himself, the fairies grew spiteful. "Is that all the thanks we get for taking you to Dublin?" they screeched. And they tried turning the girl into all sorts of different shapes

—a black dog, a bar of iron, a wool sack—but still Jamie kept hold of her. In the end, when she had regained her own shape, one of the little folk threw something at the girl.

"There's for your treachery," screamed the creature. "Now she will neither speak nor hear." Then the fairy folk flew off to their castle and left Jamie and his mother staring at the poor girl.

At first, Jamie's mother could little think how they would look after a Dublin girl who could neither speak nor hear. But they managed, as they always had done before, and soon the girl herself was helping the widow with the cooking and housework. She even helped outside, feeding the pig and the fowls, while Jamie worked away mending his fishing nets.

After a year the three had settled down together, although sometimes the girl looked sad and Jamie and his mother guessed that she was thinking of her people and her comfortable home.

When Halloween came again, Jamie decided he would

go and see the fairies once more. His mother tried to stop him, but he was stubborn, and soon he was off across the fields towards the castle.

He crept up to a window and took care not to be seen this time. Soon he heard the fairies talking about what had happened a year before. The fairy who had made the girl deaf and dumb spoke up: "Little does Jamie Freel know that a few drops of this liquid would make her better again."

Now Jamie knew what to do. He burst into the castle and stole the liquid while the little people were still welcoming him. Then he ran home and gave the girl the liquid before anyone could stop him.

The girl was happier now she could talk again, and Jamie and she decided they would go to Dublin to find her parents. After a long and arduous journey they arrived at the girl's family home. But when they knocked at the door, no one recognized her. Her parents insisted that their only daughter had died over a year ago and that they had buried her. Even when she showed them her ring, they would not believe it, accusing her of being someone who had stolen the ring and was pretending to be their daughter.

Jamie and the girl looked at each other. They realised that they would have to tell the people the story of the fairies. It was Jamie who told the story of the flight to Dublin, how the young lady was stolen, and how she had been made deaf and dumb. When he had finished, the old man and woman saw that they had been deceived and that this indeed was their daughter. They showered the girl with kisses—and embraced Jamie, too.

When the time came for Jamie to return home, the girl wanted to go too, for the pair had become inseparable. The girl's parents realised that the two should be married, and sent for Jamie's mother to come to Dublin for the grand ceremony. Afterward they were all happy, and Jamie felt that all his hard work had been richly rewarded.

Why the Manx Cat Has No Tail

In ancient times Noah was collecting together two of every animal to put in his ark. But the she-cat refused to go in before she had caught a mouse. After all, she thought, there might be no mice where she was going, and she was mad for meat.

So while all the other animals were lining up two by two, she was nowhere to be seen.

"Well," said Noah. "There will be no she-cat, and that is all there is to it."

All the other beasts were aboard, and Noah began to close the door, when up ran the she-cat. She made a great leap and squeezed through, but the closing door sliced her tail clean off.

No one bothered to mend the tail, so to this day, the cats of Man go tail-less.

But the she-cat thought it was worth it for the mouse.